TWISTED SIMULATIONS

TEN CHILLING TALES FROM THE DARK CORNERS OF THE UNIVERSE

ZACHRY WHEELER

eBook ISBN: 978-1-954153-43-1
Paperback ISBN: 978-1-954153-44-8
Hardcover ISBN: 978-1-954153-45-5
Edited by Jennifer Amon
Published by Mayhematic Press

This collection includes ten titles:
Hitchens Manor *
The Asteroid Cafe *
Calum's Descent
Bandolier
Starship Eternity
The Survey
The Claymore Incident
Noros
The Eyes of Owen
The Oxford Revelation

* Readers' Favorite® 5-Star Selections

DISCLAIMER

Twisted Simulations is a collection of short stories that probe the murky depths of science fiction. They are nonsequential and can be read in any order you please. Fair warning: the stories do not shy away from shock and gore. In fact, one might presume that the author is not right in the head.

Enjoy at your own risk.

The manor has a new owner ... and a new threat.

Two hundred years of hauntings has given Hitchens Manor a ghastly reputation. The resident ghosts have maintained a cycle of death, sale, rinse, repeat. The new owner is expected to suffer the same fate. That is, until they meet him.

HITCHENS MANOR

Hitchens Manor had many owners. It also had many murders, hangings, suicides, and suspiciously fatal accidents, making it one of the most haunted places in the world. Locals feared it, realtors hated it, and yet, it enjoyed a steady parade of purchasers. Most saw it as a grim curiosity. Others were determined to put the rumors to rest.

It all ended the same way.

Death, sale, rinse, repeat.

The 20-room mansion rested atop a grassy hill at the end of a secluded valley, making it an ideal spot for anyone looking for peace and quiet. It was built in 1789 by the Hitchens family, early pioneers of the Industrial Revolution. It stood as a testament to progress, proudly showcasing the latest building materials and techniques.

But alas, the brazen display of wealth attracted crooks, cons, and everyone in between. The family enjoyed a single year of tranquility before an unknown intruder brutally murdered them inside the home. Their bodies were found dismembered and scattered throughout the manor.

And thus began the disquietude that continues to this day.

Theories abounded, and subsequent deaths were random at best. The only thing that tied them together was the grounds of Hitchens

Manor. The floors creaked with intent. The dirt breathed with desire. Every flower was nurtured with blood.

* * *

The latest owner was due any minute, and the house staff eagerly awaited his arrival. They sat in silence around a rustic dining table inside a lavish kitchen. The butler's attire was pressed and spotless, per his usual standards. The cook wore a starched apron and her hair was pulled into a ponytail. A young gardener tended to a vase on the table. It contained a fresh bouquet of flowers that she had selected from her handiwork. Beside the vase was a food basket and a bottle of wine gifted from the realtor.

And then there was the boy.

He sat with his arms crossed and a puckered face. His role wasn't obvious, but his distaste for the moment was clear to a fault. An errand boy, perhaps. But in his current state, one wouldn't trust him to fetch the mail.

"This is taking too long," the boy said with a petulant tone.

"Patience," the butler said. "We've gone through this before and we will go through this again. No sense whinging about it."

The boy huffed dramatically.

The gardener teased a final flower and took her seat at the table.

"Gorgeous," the cook said, adding a wide smile.

The gardener grunted in response, then slouched in her chair.

The butler, ever vigilant, consulted the chain watch in his front pocket. He dared not grouse, so a quick glance and tuck was dismissed as curiosity. Moments later, the unmistakable clatter of a key-in-lock caught their attention. Their postures stiffened as the front door whined open in the distance. The kitchen was two rooms away, but the cavernous manor amplified the slightest of sounds.

Footsteps followed.

Every eye turned to the kitchen entry. The elegant trim served as a picture frame, as if to present the next master of the manor with the utmost dignity. The reveal was upon them, but they did not rise.

They remained seated at the table without much regard, as if interrupted by an unwelcome guest.

The footsteps grew louder, and louder, then stopped.

The entry remained empty, prompting confused glances around the group.

But then a head appeared.

It floated into view from midway down the frame. Short black hair and white-rimmed glasses gave the owner an urban artsy vibe. His eyes combed the space, but he ignored the staff sitting at the table. A hand slithered around the frame and up the interior wall, bringing a noodly arm with it. A slender body flowed into the kitchen like a misty apparition. The man was dressed in all black from head to toe, save for a pair of white socks that matched his glasses. He continued an intimate study of the wood-paneled wall as he prowled around the room.

"Well this is a weird one," the boy said.

The owner did not respond.

"What's wrong with him?" the cook said with a hint of concern.

"Does it matter?" the butler said. "He's here, which means our work begins." He turned to the group and smiled. "Shall we?"

The cook nodded, as did the gardener.

The boy maintained a confused stare at the intruder.

The butler reached across the table and pressed a finger to the base of the wine bottle. A gentle push nudged it closer to the edge. The rasp of glass on wood caught the new owner's undivided attention. His widened gaze whipped to the bottle, but he continued to ignore the group.

"See?" the butler said. "Every living human has that instinct." He nudged the bottle again.

The owner flinched and took a step forward, his widened gaze locked onto the bottle.

"Fear," the butler said. "The unknown." He nudged the bottle again, this time to the edge.

The owner took another step.

"The living cannot help themselves," the butler said. "Every bump a ghost. Every creak a monster." Another nudge, bringing the bottle perilously close to falling.

The owner took another step, and another, bringing him to the table. He loomed over the bottle, wearing an expression of disbelief.

"We have haunted this manor for 200 years," the butler said. "And we shall haunt it for 200 more." He nudged the bottle one final time.

But it did not fall.

The owner had thrust his hand forward to prevent a drop and shatter. An expected reaction, but with an unexpected shock. All eyes gawked at the owner's hand, not because it gripped the bottle, but because it gripped the wrist of the butler. A cold and terrible silence infected the space. The butler lifted his gaze to the owner's face, now taut with a demonic smile.

"I ... see ... you ..." the owner whispered, then grabbed the neck of the bottle and smashed the base across the ledge. As the bubbly vintage splashed the floor, the man stabbed the butler's face with savage glee. Over and over he thrust the jagged shards into his victim. Eyes popped, flesh tore, and glass scraped bone. A fountain of blood joined the sparkling wine on the floor.

The boy screamed and tumbled out of his seat.

The gardener screamed and shot backwards, scraping chair legs across the tile.

The cook screamed and desperately tried to intervene, much to the delight of the owner. He turned the bottle on the cook and raked her arms with deep gashes. She howled and flailed backwards, leaving the owner to resume his sadistic assault on the butler.

The ghosts could only watch in helpless horror as a nameless intruder mangled their cohort's flesh. The owner gripped the butler's neck and thrust him backwards. He toppled to the floor, then the owner leapt onto his chest hammered down with both hands. The vicious strikes painted the area red. The boy and gardener fled. The cook pressed her back to the wall as blood poured from her arms.

The strikes continued, coldly, fiercely, until only a slop of flesh remained. The owner, now soaked and satisfied, climbed off the lifeless butler and slithered to his feet. His crimson face slogged over to the cook, still shivering against the wall. "I ... see ... you ..." he whispered, prompting her to scream and flee the kitchen.

* * *

Later that evening, the butler was standing beside a large bed in the master suite, looming over the new owner as he slumbered. The butler's face was blemish-free, but a deep scowl was painted across it. He was a ghost, after all, so he could not suffer any permanent injury. The previous injury, however, was still of great interest to the group. No living thing had ever touched them, let alone in such a profound and disturbing way.

Thus, the butler stood over the sleeping owner, determined to get some answers.

He glanced back at the door, where the cook, gardener, and little boy stood in wait. The snafu in the kitchen had created a certain reluctance. It was a new feeling for them, a deep discomfort that they wore on their incorporeal sleeves. The very sleeves, it would seem, that their new resident psycho could yank into an unpleasant encounter.

The owner snored atop a feather pillow, blissfully unaware of the spirit standing over him. The butler sighed, then extended a finger to tap the owner's shoulder. To hell with etiquette, this harrowing incident required a stern conversation. That was the plan, if not for the mantis-like reaction of the owner. Without opening his eyes, he snatched the butler's wrist, again, and jerked him down for a face-to-face exchange.

The other three yelped in unison, then vanished down the hallway.

The butler, determined to seek clarity, gritted his teeth and awaited his fate.

The owner's right eye opened, then his left, then a sinister grin crept across his face, all while remaining on the pillow. "I ... see ... you ..." he whispered.

The butler yelped and swung at the owner with his other arm, but it passed through the man's head without contact. For a moment, the sheer insanity of the situation turned to irritation. The butler glared at his fist, then whipped his attention to the other hand, still locked inside the owner's grip. Panic set in. He snapped back as hard as he could, like a fox trying to escape a trap. But try as he might, the owner's vise-like grip kept him rooted in place.

"I ... see ... you ..." the owner whispered, then released his grip.

The butler stumbled back and fell to the floor. A backwards skitter turned into a leap and sprint. He vanished down the hallway to rejoin his frightened cohort.

The owner closed his eyes and fell back asleep.

*   *   *

The next evening, all four ghosts were hiding down in the basement. They stood in a tight circle and wallowed in deep contemplation. A pull-string light glowed overhead, illuminating old boxes, rusty tools, and numerous cobwebs. The butler tapped his chin and grunted at random. The cook gazed longingly into the dangling bulb, as if to conjure a modicum of sense. The gardener stared at the filthy floor with arms crossed. The boy sighed, fidgeted, sighed again, and fidgeted some more. His boredom was palpable, and the group ignored his not-so-subtle pleas for attention.

"Not to point out the obvious," the gardener said, "but shouldn't *he* be scared of *us?*"

"That's the usual way of things," the cook said.

"Hmph," the butler said, still in rumination.

"Maybe he's a ghost too?" the boy said.

"No," the butler said. "My hand passed right through him. He could touch me, but I couldn't touch him. Puzzling, really."

"Maybe a holy priest?" the gardener said.

"Wouldn't matter," the butler said. "Remember the exorcist?"

The group nodded and mumbled in recall.

"I completely forgot about her," the cook said with an uptick.

"She sprinted through the front door and face-planted onto the driveway."

"That was awesome," the boy said, prompting a brief chuckle from the group.

A creak overhead hooked everyone's attention. They gazed up as motes of dust detached from the rafters and floated through their bodies. More creaks followed as the owner moseyed across the living room above. His pace was slow and consistent, like a robot programmed to take its merry time.

And then came the whistles.

Faint at first, then a steady increase in volume.

The ghosts cocked their necks towards the source. They all recognized the melody, but it remained distant enough to evade detection. The creaks came to a stop, prompting nervous glances. The basement door whined open. Light flooded the stairs and the whistles gained a sudden clarity.

"Pachelbel's Canon," the gardener said.

Despite the terror of the previous evening, the group was wholly transfixed. They stared at the light, wide-eyed and petrified by sheer curiosity. The slow and steady plods of the owner turned into a slow and steady descent. His journey down the stairs created a sinister shadow along the rear wall. The whistles continued, each note accented with a heavy thump of flesh on wood. It became oddly apparent that the owner wasn't wearing any shoes.

In fact, he wasn't wearing anything at all.

As his naked body crept into the light, it became much more apparent that he was, indeed, wearing *something*. Clothing it was not, because the glistening muck that covered his body was also dripping to the floor. When he reached the bottom, he shuffled to a stop and the whistling ceased. He stared straight ahead without moving or making eye contact. White gunk slid down his legs and pooled around his feet. His gaze was blank and detached, like a zombie at rest.

And then a peculiar aroma reached the group.

The cook cringed. "Is that ... mayonnaise?"

The owner whipped his gaze to the cook, flinging a dollop of mayo onto the floor.

The ghosts flinched in unison.

"I ... see ... you ..." the owner whispered.

"How?!" the boy said, clearly miffed by the encounter.

The owner ignored him, choosing to remain locked onto the cook's terrified gaze. He grabbed a pair of hammers from a nearby workbench, then spread them out wide. Mayo dripped from his arms, creating a shadowy angel of death.

"Now see here," the butler said, "this has gone far en—"

The owner hissed and gave charge.

Screams filled the basement as metal crashed into bone. The mayo man fought with the ferocity of a rabid bear, popping skulls like grisly balloons. Blood sprayed across the interior as shrieks were silenced one by one. The attack was so swift and vicious that the ghosts could only flail in confusion. Before long, the man stood inside a circle of broken limbs, bashed faces, and creeping pools of blood.

Satisfied, he returned the hammers to the bench, now caked in brains and mayo. He turned for the stairs, resumed his whistle, and left the basement.

* * *

The next evening, the ghosts wallowed through another round of deep contemplation, this time in a greenhouse far away from the mansion. Moonlight poured through the grimy glass, highlighting a cold interior filled with pots and shelving. The boy sat atop a prep table with his legs dangling. The gardener scuffed the dirt floor beneath her boots. Despite being in her element, the discomfort was obvious. The butler stood in the center with arms crossed, definitely out of his element, and wearing his distaste for all to see. The cook sat on a filthy lawn chair with arms folded across her knees. She stared at the butler like a lost puppy, desperate for any meaningful insight.

"We all know the vague rules of ghosting," the butler said. "We can interact with surfaces. We can stand on the floor, sit in a chair, lean on a wall. We can also lightly manipulate objects. We can brush a curtain, flick a switch, nudge a bottle."

The gardener huffed. "Until a psycho stabs you to death with it."

"But everything else is spiritual, right?" the cook said. "It's all subtle."

"That's my understanding after two bloody centuries," the butler said. "We can whisper in an ear, but not yell. We can tap a ball, but not throw. And the living sure as hell can't interact with us."

"Until now," the boy said.

"So what changed?" the gardener said.

"Nothing," the butler said. "As far as I can tell."

"This is not on our side," the gardener said. "We would have sensed something. We can feel rifts and auras. Hell, even the weird voodoo lady gave us a tickle. This guy brought *nothing*."

"Maybe he *is* nothing," the boy said.

The group turned to him, intrigued.

"Like an emptiness," the boy continued. "A glitch."

"A possession," the butler said, regaining the floor. "What if this man is a meat puppet? Maybe a demon assumed control. One foot in his plane, one foot in ours."

A brief silence enveloped the greenhouse.

"Regardless," the gardener said, "I would rather not spend the next two centuries getting hammer-bashed every night."

"Or bottle-stabbed," the boy said.

The cook shivered. "I forgot what real pain felt like."

"We need a plan," the butler said.

"Uh ..." the boy said. His jittery tone hooked everyone's attention.

They turned to the boy, then followed his frightened gaze to the door. The owner stood outside. He wore a full hazmat suit with an additional gas mask beneath the visor. So consuming was the discussion that they hadn't noticed his arrival. How long he had watched was anyone's guess, not that it warranted consideration. The immediate dread had frozen everyone in place.

"I ... see ... you ..." the owner said. The mask, suit, and door were no match for the menacing tone. It reached into the greenhouse and chilled every spine present.

The boy leapt from the table and sprinted for the rear. He maintained a furious pace into the wall, fully expecting to pass through as he always had. But he did not. His tiny body slammed into the glass and ricocheted to the ground.

Panic ensued.

The cook shot to her feet and frantically searched for an escape hatch that didn't exist. Try as she might, her fate was sealed. The greenhouse had morphed into a prison cell. The gardener tried to grab a shovel, a pot, anything to hurl at the glass, but her lunging arms passed through every object. The butler, sensing the impending doom, could only stare at the owner and plead for mercy. Fear, it would seem, had finally taken root.

"Who are you?!" the butler said.

The owner did not respond.

"How are you doing this?!" the butler said.

The owner reached over to a control panel and pressed a green button. The irrigation pipes groaned and clattered as they sent their contents to the overhead misters. Moments later, a shower of tiny droplets filled the greenhouse and floated down like a humid snow. They landed on pots, shelves, glass, and much to everyone's surprise, skin. All eyes were consumed by a sudden fascination. The butler, the cook, the gardener, the boy, all stared at the tiny orbs resting on their flesh. Centuries had passed since they last felt the cool kiss of water.

The curious chill quickly morphed into searing pain.

Screams echoed through the enclosure as the acid burrowed through flesh and bone. The ghosts clawed and pummeled their own bodies, desperate to escape the agony. Chunks of sizzling meat fell to the dirt. Faces melted from skulls. The acid cut through joints and tendons, dropping entire limbs to the ground. Howls turned to garbles, then to nothing. All four were reduced to a pool of crimson goo.

The control panel pinged with completion. The misting stopped and the pipes returned to their dormant states. A final haze floated to the ground and the greenhouse fell silent once again. The owner watched as the pool belched and bubbled. It crept across the dirt like a viscous sludge. And with a final bloop, it fell silent too.

Satisfied, the owner turned away and strolled back to the house.

* * *

The next evening, the ghosts had dropped their contemplation for a plan of action. They stood in a tight group in a far corner of the garage. It was the closest they had been to the manor in days. A single SUV rested in the center of a four-car space. The owner, it would seem, was not tied to the trappings of luxury. Despite the size of the vehicle, the garage radiated emptiness. Several moths fluttered through a floodlight that shone above the entrance door.

The ghosts remained well-hidden and cloaked in darkness.

The butler, with his nose out in front, motioned to the others behind his back. They nodded, then quickly darted towards the vehicle. Each of them slipped into their respective seats without opening the doors. The butler floated into the driver's seat. The cook followed into the passenger seat. The gardener and boy filled the rear seats. And there they sat, as if awaiting a family road trip.

"This had better work," the cook said.

"And how do you know it can?" the gardener said to the butler.

"I don't," he said, then floated a hand through the steering wheel. "But you said something that got me thinking. It's as if this man creates an aura when he's around us. It breaks the rules, allows us to do things that we normally can't."

"Like drive a car," the boy said.

"Exactly. So when he comes out, we ram him with the car."

The gardener sighed. "Again, I was trapped in the greenhouse same as you, but I couldn't grab anything. Whatever the rules are, they ain't consistent."

"Then give me a better plan," the butler said, slightly miffed.

The group responded with quiet annoyance.

"Are we ready?" the butler said.

"As much as we can be," the cook said.

The other two nodded.

The butler took a breath, adjusted his posture, then lifted a single finger. He lowered it to the horn, enough to make subtle contact. And with a gentle push, a harsh blare sounded inside the garage. It was short, but enough to get the job done.

And so they waited.

The butler hovered his hands over the steering wheel, ready and anxious.

From within the house, a familiar sound needled their ears. They glanced at each other in confusion. The eerie sound barked and ceased, over and over. Each cycle a terror, each pause an eternity. And with a final drum, the sound turned into a dull rumble.

The boy gasped. "Is that ... a chainsaw?"

The dull rumble turned into a ferocious roar.

A blade pierced the entry door and chewed it from top to bottom. Dust and splinters rained into the garage. When the blade reached the base, it vanished back into the house, cueing a devastating kick from the wielder. The door shattered into shards that clattered to a rest on the concrete.

And there, standing inside the gaping hole, was a clown.

But not just any clown. This clown was dressed and painted as a living nightmare. Blood dripped from its serrated teeth. Large black patches served as eyes. Its bright red nose swam in a sea of white. A tattered suit with rainbow stripes fell to a pair of blood-soaked bunny slippers. And gripped within its jet-black gloves, was a rumbling chainsaw.

The cook screamed, prompting the butler to grip the steering wheel. And much to his surprise, the grip held. He allowed himself a bark of victory, then turned to the cook for recognition.

"What are you looking at me for?! Go, go, go!"

The chainsaw roared and the clown stepped into the garage.

The butler gritted his teeth and slammed his foot onto the gas pedal.

But nothing happened.

Victory turned to panic as he pumped the pedal over and over.

"It's not working!" the butler said.

"You have to turn it on, dingus!" the gardener said.

"How do I do that?!"

"With keys!" the boy said.

"You don't have the keys?!" the gardener said.

"You need keys?!" the butler said.

"How do you not know that?!" the boy said.

"I'm a Sixteenth Century butler!" he said, flailing his arms.

The chainsaw clown took a mighty leap forward and slammed onto the hood.

The ghosts screamed in unison and fled the vehicle. They all scampered towards the rear, where a garage door was now open. The clown had pressed the control button during the argument. Apparently, he was gunning for a chase. All four ghosts sprinted outside and towards the tree line, at which point, they abandoned all pretension of sticking together. When a chainsaw roars behind you with murderous intent, the concept of camaraderie no longer applies.

Their paths split into the forest.

The butler maintained a gangly sprint, huffing and puffing while leaping over logs. The tails of his well-pressed tuxedo fluttered behind. While not the most gifted runner, he managed to bump and stumble his way through the dense brush.

The cook yelped through her own awkward sprint. As this was a decidedly new experience, she batted away branches and cursed their existence, but her pace stayed true. Her voice bounced between rattled anger and abject terror.

The gardener, once more in her element, took to the forest like a track and field athlete. She sailed around trees and bounded over obstacles, never breaking stride. Her stony face wore a singular purpose, that of not getting murdered by an unhinged psycho (again).

The boy, despite his meager pace, managed to stay focused enough to gain distance. Fear was painted across his wide-eyed face, which he whipped over his shoulder many times. Each one found a vision of a bloodthirsty clown in pursuit. A few trips and falls resulted in hasty corrections.

And so the ghosts ran, never to return.

The clown, satisfied with this arrangement, stopped his pursuit. He bellowed with victory and roared the chainsaw overhead, one final sendoff to his unwelcome guests. The chainsaw died with a final grunt. And there he stood, alone and silent in the forest.

And then the phone rang in his pocket.

He flinched, then dutifully fished it out to answer.

"Hello, this is Jake from Fallen Angel Pest Control. How may I help you?" He paused, then nodded. "Yup, it's done. Three days and under budget. The Soldevillas can move in now." He paused again, then grunted and shook his head. "Nope, gone for good. Chainsaw clown gets 'em every time." Another nod, another grunt. "Okie doke, see you back at the office."

He spun around and whistled his way back to the house.

THE END

Kevin has a front row seat to the end of all things.

It's the off-season in lower orbit and the satellite hotels are mostly empty. But for one introvert, it's the perfect time to visit. Kevin has booked a long vacation at The Asteroid Cafe. His stay is going great, but then Armageddon ruins it all.

THE ASTEROID CAFE

The single greatest day of my life was sitting at The Asteroid Cafe, alone, watching the oceans and mountains of Earth rotate through the glass dome overhead.

And then Armageddon ruined it all.

It was the off-season for the orbital restaurant, an old fueling station converted into a basic bed and breakfast. Space tourism had reached its full stride, making satellite retrofits a popular business venture. Those with piles of cash preferred the luxurious Moon resorts, but humble dregs like yours truly could only afford the shitholes of lower orbit. It didn't bother me, to be honest. I was just happy to see the big black empty, a lifelong dream of mine.

My status as a very-not-rich person meant that I watched several missiles whiz by and slam into those lunar resorts. Not that The Asteroid Cafe was a total shithole. It had a unique charm, an edgy persona, a certain amount of ... okay, it was a shithole. A filthy, rusty, "I hope the duct tape holds" kind of shithole. But dammit, I loved every inch of it.

So yeah, there I was, sipping on a cold brewski as giant mushroom clouds lifted from the Earth and Moon. This might seem cold to admit, but I didn't have much of a reaction. The whole thing felt more curious than horrifying, as if watching an event unfold that couldn't possibly be real. It's the kind of sight that makes you question your grip on reality. Am I witnessing the end of all things, or am I uncomfortably drunk? It was only my second beer, so my brain freewheeled into outlandish explanations.

Perhaps an alien invasion.

But no ships.

Perhaps a stealth alien invasion.

But the missiles came from Earth.

Perhaps a subterranean stealth alien invasion.

Well, now you're sounding a bit silly, Kevin.

That's my name. Kevin Kyle Kane. Three first names and the worst initials imaginable. I brought this up countless times to my mother (whenever she was sober). I still maintain that she was blackout drunk when she named me, but she always denied it through a patented slur. My father didn't have any say in the matter. He skipped out during pregnancy with one of his many floozies. I only met him once, and that was twice too many. In any case, my mere existence was a gift to bullies during childhood. Is it any wonder that I ended up as a nihilistic shell of a human? But hey, at least I could watch the world burn with a straight face.

Which, as it turned out, was exactly what I was doing.

The bartender, slash waiter, slash caretaker, was in the kitchen. I was the only customer inside a four-table restaurant. In fact, I was the only customer period. I arrived on a Tuesday and hadn't seen anyone since. Aside from Burt, of course. Few people are willing to waste their vacation days aboard a floating dumpster in lower orbit. Even fewer during the off-season.

The very concept of an off-season might seem counterintuitive for an orbital holiday, given that there are no seasons in space. However, scheduled maintenance on a satellite motel is a lot more complicated than its ground-based counterpart. There's a lot of shit in orbit, and keeping it all in check is a dance with the devil. But the cost of deploying a fixit crew isn't exactly cheap, so the stations log their non-critical issues and union crews tend to them all at once.

They set aside a few months per year to address all the necessary repairs and adjustments. Teams bounce from station to station with a laundry list of honey-dos. Have you ever been asleep inside a space hostel when a course correction is issued? Warnings are for the weak, and the abrupt terror is enough to spark a massive heart attack.

Thus, the lower orbit has an off-season.

And seeing as how I hold most of humanity in contempt, it was the perfect time to visit. So there I was, drinking in the ultimate fireworks show from the glass dome above me. My brain, ever vigilant, summarized the visual with a grunt of mild interest.

"What?" Burt said as he dropped a plate of nachos on the table in front of me.

I met eyes with Burt, which required a slow detachment from my slack-jawed focus on the ceiling. One might assume that Burt would heed the cue and glance up, but one would be incorrect. Burt was a simple bloke with the social awareness of a drugged sloth. Asking him to respond to a subtle cue would be like asking a horny dog to detach from your leg. Sometimes it takes a little nudge. And so, I widened my gaze and up-nodded to the ceiling.

Burt lifted his gaze and immediately shrieked in horror. Good thing he wasn't still carrying the nachos, else I'd most certainly be wearing them. His rotund belly jiggled as he backpedaled into an adjacent table. The image stole a brief chuckle, as who can resist laughing at a burly man who suddenly drops all pretense? His bushy beard twitched and quivered as his brain replaced words with grunts and points. Before long, his eyes jerked back and forth between the nuclear annihilation and his oddly calm customer. Instead of verbalizing this concern, he spread his arms wide as if to ask *Why the fuck are you so chill?!*

I shrugged. "Not like we can do anything."

Burt pointed at the other side of the dome. "Holy Tim, they shot up the Moon too!"

"Yup."

Burt snatched his wits from the cold beyond and sneered at me. "Okay, friend. Your languidness is really disarming."

"*Languidness?* Do you even know what that means?"

"Feels right, sticking with it."

"It's ... actually right. Nicely done."

Burt smiled and basked in the small victory. But then the horrors of reality smacked his brain and he started to panic-weep. Tears pooled at the base of his sunken eyes as he scanned the carnage overhead. He cupped the back of his neck and wheezed through a deep frown.

"Family?" I said with a hint of faux empathy.

Burt nodded, maintaining eye contact with Earth.

"Sorry," I said, inserting a brief pause. "Who?"

"Floofy."

Another pause, but without the empathy. "Floofy?"

"Yeah, there's a little white rabbit who swings by my shed from time to time. I feed him cabbage from my garden. He's a good friend."

"A rabbit. In your garden."

Burt rolled his eyes. "Obviously you've never had a pet."

"Obviously you haven't either."

Burt let out a labored sigh and nodded into the bargaining stage. "He's a tough lil' bastard. Probably has a nice deep hole somewhere. I'm sure he made it." He clapped himself back to baseline, then turned to me. "How those nachos?"

Jesus fuck nuggets, what a swing. I almost admired it. I glanced at my untouched nachos and smirked. "You tell me," I said and motioned him over.

* * *

Two plates of nachos and several beers later, Burt and I mused on the implications of dying young. Well, relatively young. We were both in our mid-forties with not much to show for it. I spent most of my life hopping between shitty tech jobs while Burt spent most of his life hopping between whatever paid the bills. He actually worked as a shark hunter at one point, a reveal that garnered my undivided attention. I struggle to recall the last time I showed genuine interest in another human being, but it's impossible not to perk up when someone uses the phrase "shark hunter" in casual conversation.

In any case, we lamented our past lives as a worldwide firestorm scorched the planet. Funny enough, watching the end of the world was much like watching grass grow. Shocking, for sure, but also boring as hell. Nuclear bombs are not like firecrackers, which are over in an instant and leave you hankering for more firecrackers. Nukes are similar to massive volcanic eruptions seen from a great distance. The sheer quantity of material spewing into the atmosphere is just too great to wrap your head around, so your brain sees the event in slow motion. After a while, you're just counting the minutes until the credits roll.

We lost interest after a few hours and would glance up at the dome every so often to make sure it was still happening. World still ending? Yup. Gimme another beer. Let me know when the nuclear winter starts. And speaking of time ...

"So how long we got on this rig?" I said to Burt.

"Hmm," he said, then dropped his chin and started to mumble through the inventory. "Supply run week 'fore last, seven pallets freeze stock, two dozen barrels concentrate, two fly dudes with nowhere to be ..." Burt nodded and met my gaze. "Four years."

I flinched in surprise. "Four *years*? Are those dog years?"

"Nope. Four more birthdays, assuming the water reclaimer don't break. We won't be eating filet mignons, but that's four years of decent chow. Remember, this pod is designed to service a dozen peeps for most of the year."

"Well shit," I said, still wearing my surprise. "Good thing I like you because we're going to be roommates for a while."

A rare compliment, but I did have several beers flowing through my system. The truth was, I did like Burt. He was harmless, honest, and seemed immune to the trappings of vanity. In other words, he was easy to read and even easier to steer. And given four long years of confinement ahead of us, not wanting to murder your roommate is perhaps the best quality to have in said roommate. Which, I guess, means that I needed to get to know him more. Y'know, like a normal human being. He did respond with a toothy smile when I said I liked him, which he obviously doesn't hear much. Burt reminded me of those bumbling oddballs you meet at comic cons, the ones who are just weird enough to be off-putting, but just charming enough to dismiss as eccentric.

Not that I ever went to comic cons. I enjoy some nerdy things, but the thought of being trapped inside an auditorium with an army of middle-aged geeks is not my idea of a good time. In fact, it firmly resides in nightmare territory.

But yes, Burt. I know he befriended a wild rabbit and he used to be a shark hunter. Jeez, what a statement. That alone would be enough to sustain my fleeting interest before excusing myself to the bathroom and never seeing him again. But now I needed to dig. Ugh. I guess this is what being in prison feels like. Imagine having to find some cordial ground with a serial killer. Hmm, now that I think about it, I guess that wouldn't be too difficult.

"Y'okay?" Burt said with actual concern. "You drifted a bit."

Just thinking about murdering humans, I would have said in normal circumstances, which would have killed the conversation (pun intended again) and left me in peace. But no, I would have to mind my tongue for a while. "Just thinking about my brother," I said with a somber tone. I didn't have a brother. I had two half-sisters who needed to take flying leaps into vats of acid, but when it came to my own chore of a mother, one kid was more than enough. "He died not too long ago," I said to score some sympathy points. "I miss him, but I'm also happy that he didn't live to see this."

"Sorry," Burt said. I could tell that the statement made him a bit uncomfortable. Good to know. Empathy wasn't his strong suit. Or perhaps he never learned how.

"How about you?" I said with an uptick. "Any non-rabbit family to account for?" The joke erased the awkwardness and replaced it with a half-grin. Damn I'm good.

"Like who?"

Burt was honestly curious, which infuriated me more than it

should. Oh, I don't know, like a goddamn mother and father? Holy shit on a pogo stick. Quelling the snark was going to be a lot harder than I thought. *Oh, I don't know, like a goddamn* "mother and father?"

"Ah," Burt said with a newfound understanding. "Don't have any of those. I was given up for adoption and never met 'em. Don't even know their first names." He smiled and shrugged.

I should have felt like a dick, but I didn't. I had an info nugget, which I started tugging on like a fishhook. "What about the family that raised you?"

"Don't have any of those, either. Never got adopted, just bounced around homes until I got kicked out at eighteen." He smiled and shrugged again.

Okay, I'm not made of stone. I felt like a proper dick at that point. No wonder he ended up as a janitor in a space motel. "Wow, sorry to hear that." I paused long enough to convey some empathy, then asked the obvious question. "So how did you end up here?"

"Meh, knew a guy who knew a guy. Didn't seek it out, that's for damn sure. I don't even like being in space. But I guess I had what it took to weather this kind of life. At least, that's what Joleen told me." He eyed me to make sure I understood that Joleen was ... "My boss."

I was a bit insulted that Burt thought he needed to explain it, which opened up several more questions. But the know-thy-neighbor game was still in the early stages, so I let it slide. He had a boss, which meant that a ruleset governed the station. This added a thin layer of comfort, as many places in lower orbit were run by live-in freelancers. It was very much the Wild West of space tourism. And it should go without saying, but you didn't want to stay at an orbital motel that was owned and operated by a former fry cook. A certain amount of know-how went a very long way in the black. But anyway, back to the boss lady.

"Does Joleen own this place?" I said.

"Kind of," Burt said with an eye squint. "She and her husband manage the company that does, and they own a bunch of shares. They oversee a half-dozen stations, all of which are in good standing with the network. Her brother-in-law knows me, which is how I got the gig."

"Ah, I bet that was an interesting conversation."

"Not really. Joleen asked if I wanted to live in space. I thought, why not? Now I'm here."

Who would have thought that nabbing a space station job would be so humdrum? I was a bit disappointed, to be honest. Aside from the 'serving people' part, I struggle to conjure a better gig. "Interesting," I said with a distinct lack of interest. But hey, at least a property management company governed this shithole. "So how does that work? Do you have to check in or what?"

His eyes widened. "Shit!" Burt scrambled to his feet and jogged behind the bar. His hurried hands fumbled behind the counter for a company tablet, a coms device that allowed him to speak directly to management.

I sat at the table, unmoved, overlooking several empty plates and pints.

Burt tapped his way through a series of protocols, which ended with a sharp error ping. "Aw," he said, then lifted a foiled face. "The coms are dead."

I glanced up at the mushroom clouds and resisted the urge to mock. Ugh, being a kind and neutral human may very well be the death of me. I could only respond with a sigh and nod, but I did add a mental eye roll.

"Oh," Burt said with a sudden perk, "check this out." He wandered out from behind the counter and returned to the table. "I received an alert shortly before everything went to shit." He dropped the tablet on the table and took the seat adjacent to mine.

The screen showed a series of red-lettered data panels along with the start of a video clip. Burt ignored the info and pressed the play button, like a teenage boy neglecting his antivirus to watch a porn clip (which made me wonder what else had been ignored). The clip flickered to life and showed the bust of a middle-aged man with thick glasses and a prominent bald spot.

"That's Joleen," Burt said. "My boss," he added, just in case I didn't get it the first time.

I rolled my mental eyes.

"Attention all stations," Joleen said in a scratchy Bostonian voice. "There is an incident playing out on the ground that may have some impact on your service. All television feeds and distribution chains have been hijacked by an unknown party, which promises further info in the coming minutes. Given this uncertainty, we wanted to relay this feed to you, should it result in any disruptions. Rest assured that we are on top of the situation."

I glanced up at the scorched planet.

Joleen looked off-screen and argued with a colleague about the start of the live feed. They exchanged some choice words, then Joleen grunted and returned to the camera. "The feed is starting," he said. "Hold tight, back in a bit."

I glanced up at the scorched planet again.

The tablet flickered over to a black screen with a white logo. The depiction of a naked baby holding a pair of machetes was more curious than fearsome. Burt and I traded confused glances before a counter ticked down from ten. When it reached zero, the screen faded to a clean-cut gent wrapped in an orange robe. He wore thin glasses and a creepy smile that screamed "free candy." His teeth were straight, his hair was neat, and his body was average, like a tech support guy in a monk costume.

"Greetings, people of Earth," he said with a meek voice and open arms.

Not a terrorist.

A religious crackpot.

Who was likely a terrorist.

Splitting hairs, really.

"My name is Jersona'ra, Supreme Leader of the Taronan Church of Healing."

I bet his real name was Jason. He looked like a Jason.

"I come to you with blessed news," he said, then cracked an even weirder smile. "Today, we all become one with Zorloth the World Maker, architect of our planet and the universe beyond. 'Tis a glorious day, brothers and sisters. Fear not. You need only open your heart to the great cleansing. In a few moments, we will fuse with Him, who is She, and It shall deliver us from the torment of existence."

A robed arm reached into the frame and handed the supreme leader a remote device, complete with a radio antenna and a big red button.

"Huh, wonder what that does," Burt said.

I closed my eyes and swallowed the snark.

The leader cradled the device to his chest and hovered a thumb over the button. His widened eyes and creepy smile returned to the camera. "On my mark," he said, addressing a network of cohorts around the world. "We are one. We are Zorloth. Three ... two ... one ... " He pressed the big red button and the feed went dead.

I sighed and shook my head.

Burt looked confused, but then a rush of realization broke through the haze. "Holy schnapps, *they* did this!"

"That's a sharp deduction." My sarcastic tone floated right over Burt's head.

"But why?"

"Why do nutjobs do anything?"

Burt awaited an actual answer.

"Because they're nutjobs."

"Oh."

I leaned back in my chair and stared at the chaos above. "A merry band of religious kooks delivering the apocalypse on live television. Must admit, that was not on my 'ways to die' bingo card." I grabbed my near-empty pint of beer and tossed back the remainder.

"I thought it would be space cancer."

My gaze slogged over to Burt, which prompted him to continue.

"You see, it's like regular cancer, but when dark matter radio waves hit metal siding, it causes a massive conduction of—"

I raised my hand, cutting off what was sure to be a tangled web of conspiracy theories.

Burt nodded. "Another time then."

We sat in silence for a bit, digesting the stupidity of the predicament. Everything we knew was gone, all for some wacko pipedream of becoming one with nothing. Granted, I didn't *love* much of anything and humans disgusted me at a baseline. But I did like ... hummus. Dammit, humans made great hummus. And I'll never taste that delicious nutty treat ag—

"Wait," I said to Burt. "Do you serve hummus?"

"What's hummus?"

And I'll never taste that delicious nutty treat again.

* * *

To understand the glorious folly we found ourselves in, one must first understand the unregulated chaos of the Lower Orbit Gold Rush. This was not an official period, just a nickname coined by a bunch of greedy assholes. "Gotta get that LOGR green," was a common refrain from reckless opportunists who had no business running a lemonade stand, let alone a space station. You see, when someone opens a restaurant on the ground, it must satisfy a smorgasbord of regulations within the country it occupies. The vacuum of space is governed by fuck-all, so anyone with a rocket, hope, and a prayer can put an air-tight box in orbit and call it a day spa.

When meeting a caretaker aboard an orbital vessel, one would rightly expect them to possess a grade school understanding of astrophysics. Or at the very least, mechanics or engineering. But sadly, Burt was the norm, not the exception.

Did I mention he used to be a shark hunter?

I was a freelance programmer.

Yup, we were baristas on a submarine.

The only consolation was that everyone in orbit was in the same boat. I imagine they all watched the end of the world through their own portholes, complete with gushing tears and horrified faces. Burt and I had the advantage of emotional detachment. We started assessing inventory while everyone else was in existential shock. It wasn't long before we saw our first "this isn't a life worth living" corpse float by the glass dome. The first of many. I guess I could understand the sentiment, but it's not like we were running from a wall of fire on the ground. We had cold beer, warm beds, and plenty of food stores, so leaping into the frozen vacuum of space seemed like an overreaction.

The big unspoken question was, "How the fuck does anyone get back to Earth?" (After the nuclear fallout, of course.) The unspoken answer was, "Your question is dumb and I hope you like your orbital tomb." Nobody was qualified to work the problem and it's not like these stations had flight manuals or escape pods. We were adrift inside a high-stakes game of bumper cars, where survival depended on *not* bumping into anything.

But anyway, Burt and I made sure that the station was in full working order (to the best of our limited abilities). We checked supplies, ran diagnostics, and told the navigation AI to "keep your shit together." It seemed to understand, so we settled in for a well-earned lounge. Not much else to do but play cards and count corpses, so that's exactly what we did.

* * *

"Gin!" Burt said with a wide smile, then dropped his hand face-up on the table. He reached into the center and grabbed a candy bar from a small bucket. I'm still not sure what the rules were that denoted a sugar snatch, but we didn't care. We weren't even keeping score.

"That's two in a row," I said and downed the last sip of beer. "Going for the hat trick?"

"I don't like hats, much less magic tricks. Makes my hair itchy. The hat, not the magic." Burt added a shrug, as if the statement somehow warranted sympathy.

"Anyway," I said while grabbing the deck to shuffle, "you want to get another round while I tee up your third win?"

"Sure," Burt said. He swiped my bottle and rose to his feet. "Y'know, there should be a cool name for three wins in a row." He nodded with sudden contemplation, then turned to fetch some frosties. His brain would work the problem and I assumed that some barking answers would—

"Trio-fer!" Burt said from afar.

—would greet my ears in short order.

"Threesome!"

I snorted. "That one's taken." Maybe it was the absurdity of the situation coupled with the absurdity of the company, but I cracked a genuine smile. "Let's just call it a Burtriple."

"Oooo, I like that," Burt said as he returned with two cold bottles. He clunk-slid one across the table and reclaimed his seat.

I had already started to deal the next hand. The cold silence of the station interior meant that we could hear every card whisp across the table. Burt munched through a candy bar with one hand while his other hand snatched each individual card that arrived. Every reveal was met with a grunt of obvious delight or disappointment. If this was a poker table, I would have cleaned out his bank account. I dropped the deck in the center and picked up my hand. Burt hummed to himself as he organized his cards. I used the lull to reach across the table and snatch his beer. He barely registered the slight, content to rearrange his hand like a confused toddler.

"The fuck is this?" I said, studying the label.

"Dunno," he said. "I just drink what they send me."

I leaned forward for a closer inspection. "Smells like a bock."

"What are you, the beer police?"

"Just curious," I said and slid it back to his side. "I like interesting brews. Mine is a Belgian Dark. See, you can tell by the—"

Burt glared at me.

"You don't care. Okay then, start us off."

Burt grabbed a card from the center and added it to his hand. He thought for a moment, took a sip, and placed a card in the discard pile. "Did you ever have any life goals?"

"What, like shark hunting?" I said, taking a card.

Burt chuckled. "No, like, open a business, start a family. That kind of stuff."

"I'm not sure I'm drunk enough for this." I tossed a card onto the pile.

Burt snatched a card. "I wanted to be an astronaut."

The statement caught me off-guard. I couldn't laugh or poke fun, I just let it linger as a plain and simple statement. "Not to point out the obvious," I said, then pointed at the glass dome above us.

Burt laughed into a cough. "No, not like that. Like, real deal. NASA and whatnot." He wiped some sweat from his forehead and dropped a trio of sevens face-up. A discard followed.

I grabbed the discard and added it to my hand. "That's kinda sweet," I said with a hint of reverence. "I guess we all wanted that grandiose adventure as kids."

"And what about you?" Burt said.

I thought for a moment, then dropped a series of spades. "My grand aspiration was actually quite simple." I plucked a card from my hand, lowered it to the pile, then locked onto Burt's curious gaze. "I wanted to write a sophisticated computer worm that could infiltrate nuclear silos without detection. And then, I wanted to give its activation protocol to the craziest people on the planet."

Burt grappled with the notion for a moment, then the smile faded from his face.

"And then," I continued, "I would flee to lower orbit and watch the end of civilization with a beer in hand." I raised my bottle and grinned. "Gotta love the off-season."

"You?" Burt said with a soft and bewildered tone. His gaze lifted to the nuclear annihilation. He gasped into a sudden coughing fit. After several barks and heaves, he re-met my gaze across the table. "*You* did this?" His eyes pleaded to make sense of it all.

I shrugged. "Let's just say that I have elevated my distaste for humanity to the highest possible level. In fact, my ultimate goal is to be the last set of human eyeballs to gaze upon the planet. Nobody is going to survive this nuclear winter. And given the current stocks of The Asteroid Cafe, I have a very good shot of reaching that goal."

Burt rose from his seat, never breaking eye contact. His burly frame towered over the table, like a bully looming over a group of nerds. I wasn't sure what he intended, but his clenched fists provided a clue. Our friendship, it would seem, was nearing its end. Luckily for my face, a sudden bout of illness stole his attention and he reached for his throat. His chest swelled, his knees buckled, and he collapsed to the floor. Fluid gurgled inside his throat, sending a grim melody through the sterile air.

"Cyanide," I said.

Burt, now writhing on his back with white foam oozing from his mouth, met my gaze for a few brief seconds. It was a moment of pain and recognition, a sense of clarity known only to the damned. He knew that I had poisoned his beer. It was subtle sleight of hand that even a bad magician could master. It made Burt wonder, during his agonizing exit, how many people had preyed upon his trust. I was proud of Burt, my amusing and temporary companion. Maybe he wasn't so slow after all.

"It works quickly," I said as a morbid comfort.

He didn't respond. Burt stared up into the black abyss until his final moment. His body stopped moving, the station went silent, and I finished the rest of my beer.

"Make that *eight* years of supplies," I said to his lifeless corpse.

I stood up, grabbed his ankles, and dragged him towards the airlock.

THE END

To escape prison, one must first escape reality.

Calum has been locked inside a moon prison for thirteen years. The days are long, the future is bleak, and his mind has reached a breaking point. It's time to escape. But to do so, he must confront a living nightmare.

CALUM'S DESCENT

A lone man stood inside an empty room with a pistol in one hand and a cross in the other. The pistol dangled at his side and trembled in a fearful grip. It was a military-grade plasma weapon with exceptional stopping power. The cross was pressed to his chest. It was made of two wooden dowels, bound together with strips of fabric ripped from his prison cot.

But a prisoner he was no more.

The man lingered around a large black panel on the floor. He stared at it with an intense trepidation, pleading for courage, yearning for the strength to proceed. The room was round, eerily silent, and filled with sterile light. There were no ports or windows, only a single door that vanished into the smooth walls. The towering interior trapped the man like a bug in a jar.

Seamless white panels surrounded him from floor to ceiling. The black panel in the center dominated the space, serving as a menacing outlier. It was a few meters wide with a glowing red perimeter. The man drew a deep breath, then exhaled a potent mixture of fear and faith.

One step.

One step and his sentence was over.

And so he took it.

"Descent activation commenced," said a synthetic voice.

The red perimeter turned green, cueing a loud clunk beneath the man's feet. It startled him. He had watched this moment a thousand times, but the horrid sensation chilled him to the bone. His chest swelled as a profound sense of loss infected his mind.

"Ten seconds," the voice continued.

His breathing quickened.

"Five seconds."

Sweat.

"Four."

Salt.

"Three."

Acid.

"Two."

"Forgive me," he said with a whimper.

"One. Descent activated."

The panel detached and began its slow plunge into the abyss.

The man held his breath as a sudden dread needled his skin. Lighting strips crept past his vision, creating a searing anticipation that forced his eyes shut. His grips tightened on the gun and cross. They promised freedom, and were equally culpable in its loss.

The hum of descent slithered through his legs and up to his sweating scalp. After an agonizing minute, the panel pressed into his soles and the humming ceased. His eyes opened as a metal pane slid overhead and latched, sealing off the shaft. As silence returned, his attention shifted to the large door in front of him. A heavier clunk broke the brief calm. The door rumbled open, revealing the hellscape that had fed his nightmares for so many years.

A cloud of hot and humid air choked his lungs. Try as he might, the man could not resist coughing through the onslaught. Not a great start. But then again, stealth wasn't much help in the caves of eternity. He was there, and they knew it.

Contact imminent.

Time irrelevant.

Current prep would have to do.

As if to goad his resolve, a piercing shriek echoed from deep within the hollow.

The man shuddered, then stepped onto a damp surface of black stone. The craggy cavern was much larger than the white room. Numerous tunnels littered the walls like dots on a canvas, all of which he had seen before. Dim lights traced the entrances with faint outlines. They all stared back at him, like the black pupils of a multi-eyed monster.

Another shriek echoed from within, hastening his will.

The plan was simple.

Pick a cave and run.

And so he did.

The soles of his boots slapped the wet rock as he sprinted down a random passage. Another shriek quickened his pace. He scuffed around corners and sailed through junctions, picking new paths without thought or hesitation. Tunnel lights sailed overhead, giving his eyes just enough detail to keep pace. His lungs swelled. His muscles ached. Adrenaline pumped through his body.

And then another shriek erased it all.

So loud.

So close.

He skidded to a halt and whip-aimed the pistol down an adjacent tunnel. Silence returned. Widened eyes scanned the passage, hunting for any signs of movement. A shifting shadow stole his attention and yanked his arm into a burst of plasma fire. Multiple streaks hit the wall with flashes of blue light, sending a shower of pebbles into the cavern. The blasts echoed through the cave system, alerting everything inside to his presence.

Panic took root.

Then came the pain.

A sudden, burning, shooting pain at the base of his leg.

The beast had sunk its claws deep into the man's calf. It had ducked into a flanking tunnel to attack its prey from behind. The man screamed and crumpled to the ground. The beast gripped the bone beneath the flesh and galloped down the tunnel, dragging away its catch. The man howled as his body skidded along the craggy rock. Cloth ripped like paper. Flesh tore from his frame.

Still gripping his final testaments, he pressed the cross to his chest and fired the pistol at his captor. Bolts of plasma streaked through the cavern. A few managed to hit the beast, but careened off its thick carapace. No reaction. In a moment of pure desperation, the man pressed the barrel to his knee and blasted through the flesh. Each shot released a spray of blood and a wail of pain. And with a final pull of the trigger, freedom returned.

The man lay battered and shredded as a pool of blood widened beneath him. He coughed up a dollop of blood, then glanced down at his mangled stump. Instinct forced his hands to cover the wound, but the amassed pain of broken bones and deep gouges kept him flat.

He did, however, meet eyes with the beast.

It stood on all four legs a few meters away. Puffs of heated breath fled its slender nostrils. Multiple eyes caught reflections from the tunnel lights. The milky white orbs cut through the gloom, like glistening marbles embedded in armor.

"You're new," the man said with a gargled strain.

The beast stepped forward through a faint beam of light, revealing the countless stumpy horns that covered its body. Its sluggish approach prompted the man to raise the pistol, but the previous chaos had failed his grip. A fumbling search was cut short when the beast pinned the man's arm beneath its blood-soaked mitt. The man swallowed a whimper as giant claws dug into flesh and rock. His lungs emptied. The dream ended and reality bared its teeth.

"Go on then," the man said.

The beast leaned forward, giving the man just enough reach to jab the cross into one of its eyes. The orb popped. Black fluid spilled from the socket and onto the man's chest. He expected a brief reprieve to find the pistol, but the beast did not flinch. Instead, a new milky orb tunneled through the flesh and re-met the man's gaze. The beast stood its ground without fear or pain.

The man fell limp. The cross clattered to a rest on the rocky ground. Resignation flooded his body and he welcomed the grand exit. But the beast, now curious, refused to give it to him. It stepped back and observed the man, as if to goad its prey into another chase. The man gawked at the beast, then frantically scanned the cave for any sliver of hope. A faint glimmer caught his attention. It rested on the ground a few meters away.

The pistol.

Flipping onto his chest, he clawed through his own blood to reach salvation.

The beast did not react.

After several agonizing pulls, the man gripped the pistol with a maimed hand and spun to the beast. His trembling arm summoned the strength for a single shot. It missed. Another shot bounced off its hide like a rock skimming a pond. The beast galloped forward and sank its dagger-like teeth into the man's shoulder. A savage yank ripped the arm from the socket. The man screamed into a bloody gurgle. The beast remained curious, standing over its prey with arm in mouth.

The man begged for death.

But instead, more eyes appeared in the darkness. The beast dropped the arm and stepped aside, allowing its curious brethren to partake. The man survived for several minutes, and his wails of agony echoed through the caverns for the duration.

* * *

That death was particularly gruesome, even for an audience of hardened criminals. The scene was playing on a loop inside every prison cell, and had been since the day it befell. Eighty-one days in total, an eternity inside the complex. The inmates understood that a crueler death meant a crueler wait. It was often said that anyone could get used to anything, given enough time. But this grisly death was actively challenging that assertion.

"I guess my birthday is as good a day as any," Cal said while staring at the ceiling of his prison cell. He lay on a basic cot along the rear wall. His arms were crossed atop his chest, as if to meditate on the coming events of the day.

The day, as it were.

He sighed and glanced at the hologram feed that filled the adjacent wall. Another loop of revulsion, another knot in the stomach. His gaze continued around the cramped confines, his home of 13 years. It was a white box of concrete no more than a few meters in each direction. A cot, a desk, and a toilet amounted to a fully furnished cell. The metal bars of an entry door offered the only contrast to the stark interior. He knew every crack, every chip, some of which he had put there himself.

His eyes locked onto a particular crack. The paint came off rather easily, he recalled. The skin on his hand also came off easily. He broke six bones that day, but not before creating that tiny blemish. It was a small victory, one that he came to cherish many years later.

"Perhaps fists will be my choice," he said, then immediately scoffed at the notion. "No. I need precision. Power and precision."

A harsh buzz echoed through the corridor. It startled him during the first several months, but he quickly grew accustomed to it. He could practically guess the second, as the complex was governed by a strict schedule that hadn't changed since the day he arrived. Routine, it would seem, was an integral part of compliance.

He climbed to his feet and shuffled towards the door. It unlocked and whined open, as it always had. Thirty of his fellow inmates walked outside and gripped the railing in front of them. A collection of gray jumpsuits created the image of an impending seminar, which never came. Electrodes within the railing counted every soul present. There were always a few stragglers, by old age or heavy slumber. They all waited in silence for the chime of confirmation, signaling the coming breakfast. In a world gripped by docket, it offered the only true anticipation.

Save for this day.

This terrible and beautiful day.

Cal glanced around a large open space that split the complex from ground to ceiling. His cell was on the third level of a five-level wing. Each floor contained 30 cells with guard posts and perimeter walks. Every hand remained glued to the railing as security drones hovered through the space. Inmates traded tired glances. A few sighs broke the silence as they awaited the chime. Cal met eyes with his longtime neighbor, a meaty chap with a long white beard.

"Happy birthday," the man mouthed with little fanfare.

It was a yearly tradition that annoyed Cal, as the ticking clock needed no reminder. But on this day, the gesture hit him with an unexpected sincerity.

Cal smiled and nodded.

His gaze fell to the bottom floor, where several guards hunted for dysfunction. An empty spot along the second-floor railing had seized their focus. It belonged to an elderly man who struggled with arthritis. More often than not, it was he who delayed breakfast. A security drone darted to the area and shined a spotlight into the cell. The man's brittle frame shuffled out shortly after. He gripped the railing, cueing the familiar chime.

And so the days went.

Every inmate turned towards the exit at the far end of the corridor. Like a well-practiced dance, they commenced a slow trudge towards the cafeteria. Cal followed his neighbor down the walkway, as he had countless times before. Security drones hummed and chirped as they scanned for abnormalities. Inmates treated them with cautious indifference, as it took a true act of defiance to trigger a hostile response. Said response, though, was truly hostile. The drones carried enough firepower to tear a body to shreds, a brutal reality that Cal had witnessed during his decade of captivity.

The entire wing was emptied in less than a minute. Cal, residing near the end of his row, always counted the seconds it took to reach the exit. The average was 42, a figure that he re-calculated every morning. And 42 it remained.

Inmates descended flanking stairwells to form a single line at the ground floor. The line snaked through the primary exit and into a massive corridor, where it merged with a dozen other wings. Guards tromped along a suspended platform several meters overhead. It clung to a domed ceiling that stretched for half a mile, ending at a facility hub that included the cafeteria.

The distance served two main purposes. First, the walks to and from meals doubled as daily exercise, a foundational challenge when living on a remote moon. Building it into routine was a lot cheaper than building dedicated facilities. And second, it allowed time and distance should anything escape. The things in question remained a mystery. Inmates were not privy to any pertinent intel. Speculations abounded, but rarely found much conversation. Watching the feeds was horrifying enough.

Twelve lines of prisoners marched down the corridor like troops to battle. But unlike troops, there wasn't much spirit or synchrony. Countless soles rapped along the concrete floor. Guards continued to clank overhead as drones floated in pace with the gray battalion.

Cal glanced at a drone as it passed overhead. It carried a scratch from when it bumped into a supply cart, earning it the nickname Derp. Cal smiled at Derp and gave it a wave, to which it responded with a sudden target lock. The drone whipped towards Cal and locked its gaze to his. A single red eye glowed with violent intent as it scanned Cal from head to toe. After a few tense seconds, it dropped the lock and floated away, deeming him unlikely to cause a ruckus.

Cal's neighbor glanced over his shoulder. *What was that about?* he asked without saying a word.

Nothing, Cal responded through a grin and shrug.

A few minutes later, the marching mass entered a large open dome. An enormous grid blinked to life across the floor, representing the total population of the complex. Each meter-wide square featured a wing and cell number. The mass dispersed and each inmate searched for their corresponding spot. Before long, all 1,800 prisoners had settled inside the space.

Cal glanced at his cell neighbor, now to his immediate right. The large brute maintained a forward stare, no doubt impatient for breakfast. Cal let his gaze wander the giant dome. Several passages led to various facilities. Drones floated to their assigned posts within the chamber. The upper walkway split in two and wrapped around the perimeter, meeting at a large platform in the rear.

A stoic figure stood atop the platform with arms locked behind his back. He loomed over the space with lieutenants to either side. A dark green uniform featured gold trim and several bars of rank. It created an air of command that no one dared to question. His steely gaze combed the assembled inmates. He drew a heavy breath, then unlocked his arms and bellowed into the chamber.

"Ten days it's been," he said in a gruff voice. "Is there no bravery among the wicked? Most of you would slit my throat if given the chance, yet none of you have the courage to claim your freedom." He released a heavy sigh and shook his head. "You are here because the universe has rejected you. You are scum, miscreants, filthy demons who contaminate the civilian world. But that's *their* world. *Your* world has yet to be discovered. Need I remind you that the freedom you so desire is yours to take? You need only accept the brutality of its acquisition."

Silence responded.

The commander raked a disgusted gaze across the group, then refolded his arms and turned to leave. He nodded to one of his lieutenants, who heeded the call and stepped up to the railing. A hologram panel manifested beside him, mirroring the grid below. He consulted a few data points, then cocked his chin and cleared his throat.

And so began the grimmest of rituals.

"Attention all inmates," he said. "The time has come to claim your independence. Penal Colony Addis is now accepting volunteers for Descent. Present yourselves for immediate consideration."

The memories of armored beasts galloped through every mind.

After a cold stillness, a single hand rose from the crowd.

The square beneath Cal's feet began to glow.

A matching square on the hologram pinged with selection. It summoned an inmate profile, which the lieutenant dutifully scanned. Vitals good. Cognition good. Green across the board. An ironic validation, given what it granted.

"Inmate 84592," the man said, then eyed Cal deep within the crowd. "Do you accept the risks of Descent and volunteer to participate of your own volition?"

"I do," Cal said.

"Request approved. Proceed to processing."

A door beneath the platform clanked and slid open.

Cal glanced at his longtime neighbor, who stared back at him through a pained expression. In that woeful and wordless moment, they had crossed the mental desert into friendship. It was a brotherly bond that would never be. Cal nodded at the man, then turned away forever.

Murmurs lifted from the gathered mass as Cal stepped towards the front. Several hands patted his back along the way. They signaled respect, or at the very least, a thankful reset of the current feed. Cal exhaled a fluttering breath as the weight of the decision crushed his calm. His eyes shift back and forth, meeting the final gazes of all he passed.

Cal exited the mass and proceeded alone. His eyes lifted to the platform where the cold glares of bondage watched his every step. The plods of his boots echoed through the silent chamber. The door to oblivion seemed to widen, as if hungering for its next victim. He passed through the frame and glanced back at the gathering.

And with a slide and clank, they were gone.

Cal found himself inside a short hallway with another door at the end. It slid open, revealing a small white room with a dressing bench in the center. It was the only part of Descent that Cal had never seen. The feed always began at weapon selection, and every inmate was grimly curious as to what transpired beforehand. Now he knew. It would seem that changing room modesty also applied to moon prisons in remote galaxies.

He stepped into the room and the door slid shut behind him. The space wasn't much bigger than his prison cell. Seamless panels created a perfectly smooth box in which to brood. The bench in the center was welded to the floor, no doubt to dissuade any fits of violence. The opposite wall was backlit with sterile light, illuminating a faint checkered pattern. Cal recognized them as clothing alcoves, the same ones he used when it was time to refresh his prison duds.

One of them glowed with a green hue. He stepped forward and pressed his hand to the panel. It scanned his biosignature and pinged with confirmation. The panel slid open, revealing a fresh set of clothes. Only this time, the soft gray jumpsuit had been replaced with hardened leather. He scooped the ensemble and carried it over to the bench for inspection.

Long-sleeve undershirt.

Leather tunic, synthetic, firm yet pliable.

Same for the pants.

Double stitching, no pockets.

And a pair of rugged boots.

Cal grunted with satisfaction, an unexpected reaction given the circumstances. He recalled a similar garb from his distant past. The only thing missing was a proper helm. But knowing what awaited, he was grateful for the gift.

A subsequent ping caught his attention. He turned to the adjacent wall to find a large glowing panel. The next door. A hologram timer began counting down from one hour. A smaller waist-high panel opened nearby, revealing a hot steaming breakfast on a plastic tray. But it wasn't the standard prison breakfast of scrambled protein. These were eggs, *real* eggs, cooked by a knowing hand. The meal was complete with toast, bacon, and a tall glass of orange juice.

Cal stared at the delectable treat in woeful disbelief. The reality of the situation, ever-present and apparent, suddenly gained tremendous gravity. Get dressed, enjoy your last meal, in your last hour of peace, then confront death with reckless abandon. The aroma of sizzling pork tickled his nostrils. He stepped over to the cubby, plucked a piece of bacon from the tray, and crunched through a moment of pure happiness. A flood of long-forgotten memories prompted a chuckle.

The first ten minutes were utter bliss. Every bite a pleasure, every chew a rapture, every moan a call to better times. He carried the tray over to the bench and took a seat, where he patiently finished the meal and licked the plate clean. The orange juice remained untouched, but not for lack of desire. It was a prize worth waiting for.

The sweet tingle of citrus would conclude the best meal of the past decade. He lifted the sweating glass and savored every drop, slowly, deliberately. With a final toss, he closed his eyes and groaned with deep satisfaction.

"Kill me now," he said quietly, then glanced at the ticking clock.

Forty-five minutes.

He sighed and got on with it.

Dressing would not kill as much time as he hoped, even after neatly folding his jumpsuit and returning it to the cubby. Pacing failed to offer the usual reprieve, as his prison cell did not contain a ticking doom clock. As much as his mind yearned to wander, it snapped back with every pop of leather. Before long, he accepted the preoccupation and settled on the bench facing the door. Prep, and only prep, consumed his final thoughts.

"Power and precision," he said again.

And again.

And again.

"Five minutes until weapon selection," said a synthetic voice.

It was the same voice that had needled his ears for years. Cal had watched countless Descents from the confines of his cell. He knew the words. He knew their grim significance. But hearing them over-head, and in that particular space, filled him with a unique and biting tension. The commencement had echoed through every cell in the complex, and all eyes would be on him in less than five minutes. Per-haps it was performance anxiety, maybe a pang of shyness. Whatever it was, the sudden need to vomit was too much to handle. The delec-table last meal turned into a puddle at his feet. His face softened as he stared into the muck, somewhat miffed by his frightful stomach. It turned into a welcome distraction, as the last minutes ticked away with his eyes buried in chunky regret.

A buzzer sounded, hooking Cal's gaze to the door. The clock showed zero and the panel faded, along with every light in the room. Cal stared into the darkness, a ghastly void of his own making. The sudden stillness calmed his nerves and recentered his focus.

"You now have five minutes to select a weapon for Descent,"

said the voice.

The door slid open.

Sterile light poured into the dressing room.

And there it was.

Four walls, each filled with gleaming tools of destruction. Blades, barrels, bludgeons, every shape of metal imaginable. They hung inside backlit cubbies that spanned from floor to ceiling. Cal rose from the bench and stepped inside the arsenal. The door slid shut behind him, concluding the prelude. He scanned the interior with a cold intensity. Hidden cameras beamed his every move to a captive audience. He knew the feed had started, but his training demanded focus.

"Power and precision," he said one last time, igniting the hunt.

Too big.

Too small.

Too slow.

Too heavy.

And then his prize revealed itself.

"There you are," he said to a familiar companion. He recognized it from boot camp. He recognized it from the battlefield. He even recognized it from his bedroom closet. The pulse rifle was a special ops weapon that blurred the line between soldier and assassin. As one such operative, it had saved his life on numerous occasions. This was a newer model, but it retained the same stock and build.

Only idiots try to improve perfection.

He lifted the rifle with both hands, balancing the weight between them. The cold metal was foreign yet familiar. He rolled it to the side, revealing a yellow bar that denoted full charge. The weapon fired bursts of electrostatic that sliced through flesh and armor like tiny lightning bolts.

Cal inspected the rifle with deliberate hands. His brain summoned a flurry of recollection. Sprays of blood, intense standoffs, and of course, victory. Muscle memory was swift and tactical. He launched into maneuvers, stances, readiness, everything a seasoned soldier needed to survive.

"Please proceed to Descent," said the voice.

Another door opened, revealing a familiar round room with white walls and black floor panel. Cal could see the dark square from inside the armory. The glowing red perimeter hooked his eye like a moth to the flame. The entire prison held its breath. Cal filled his lungs with the dread of a thousand men. His eyes closed in fear, then reopened with purpose.

Freedom or death.

He surged forward with a brash confidence seldom seen inside the complex. Step by step, he embraced his fate with a disarming calm. Cal crossed the perimeter and planted his feet on the black panel, as if to thumb his nose to the reaper. He tucked the pulse rifle into his armpit and softened his knees, well before the platform clunked beneath him. Dormant training flooded his veins, transforming his body into a battle-ready machine. He was staring into the Maw of Deraguun. He was standing on the Peak of Ky Rath. He was ready.

And so it began.

"Descent activation commenced," said the voice. "Ten seconds."

Cal tightened his grip as the ghostly overseer counted down to an unknown fate. His gaze remained forward-focused, primed to guide him through the chaos. Freedom awaited. True freedom. And all he had to do was sprint through the shadow of death.

The countdown concluded and the platform began its slow plunge. Lighting strips passed through his vision, but he did not waiver. Every controlled breath fortified his resolve. Whatever horrors greeted him, he would meet them head-on with courage and conviction.

A dull pressure hit his feet.

An overhead panel slid shut.

Descent concluded with an ominous clunk.

And for a moment, Cal basked in the solitude.

"Knees and head," he said under his breath. "Bacon bread." The old mantra looped inside his head, goading him to survive at all costs. It cleared the mind and boiled every thought down to war. Kill to live. Kill to win. Kill for absolution.

The door slid open.

But the mouth of Hell did not reveal itself.

Cal remained poised for combat while staring into a large white room. A round room with seamless panels, like the one he had departed. Resting at the center was a thick wooden desk. And sitting behind it was a man in a three-piece suit.

"Calum McCready," the man said, then checked his tablet. "Inmate 84592 of Penal Colony Addis, sentenced to life for triple murder."

Cal blinked a few times, trying to offload the hallucination. He took a cautious step forward and peeked into the sterile room. The rifle remained tucked and ready, should the obvious deception become apparent. Nothing abnormal met his gaze, apart from the wholly unexpected presence of a suited man and a desk.

"Self-defense," Cal said.

"Come again?"

"It was self-defense," Cal said again, this time with a notable disdain. "But I guess that doesn't matter when you kill the son of a magnate."

"It's noted in your record."

"And yet here I am."

"And yet here you are." The man smiled and folded his hands atop the desk. "Speaking of which, we need to discuss your pending release."

Cal stammered a bit, then tightened his grip. "What the hell is this?"

"It's your release hearing."

"My rel—" His flustered gaze bounced around the chamber. "Where are the caves?"

"There are no caves."

Cal locked eyes with the man.

"The feeds are AI-generated," the man continued. "In fact, yours is currently rolling." The man tapped his tablet and a hologram feed appeared above the desk. It showed Cal in a cavern sprint with a pair of monsters in pursuit. He skidded to a halt, turned to aim, and placed a flurry of bolts into the knees of the charging beast. It buckled and fell, which also tripped the one behind it. Cal lined up a pair of headshots and dispatched them both. Another monster shrieked from afar, which yanked him back into a sprint. "You're doing quite well," the man said, adding a toothy smile.

Cal lowered his weapon and stepped towards the desk, transfixed by his own death run. His widened eyes studied every stride, every twitch, every quirk of familiar movement. It was a perfect recreation. Cal had walked through the uncanny valley and entered a dream, one that he could not recall.

"How is this possible?" he said.

"The system has been watching you nonstop for 13 years. It also has footage from your military ops. It knows you better than you know yourself. In fact, it has determined that you will be the first successful runner since 76409. So congrats on that. You will provide some much-needed inspiration."

Cal met eyes with the man. "Inspiration?"

"We need more Descents. The last feed was a bit much for the collective psyche. Granted, we had already fulfilled our quota for several months, but now we're short. The system did not anticipate such a strong reaction. It was a glitch."

"A *glitch*? We watched a man get ripped apart, on loop, for *months*."

"Got you here, didn't it?"

Cal raised the pulse rifle and shot a flurry of bolts into the man's head. They sliced through the hologram image and hit the rear wall, creating a series of charred impacts. Cal glanced down at the weapon, then back to the man, who remained calm and unblemished behind the desk.

"Now *that* would have been murder," the man said.

Cal huffed, then dropped the rifle to his side and released his grip. The weapon clattered to a rest on the floor. He began to pace aimlessly as his mind struggled to make sense of the predicament. The man waited patiently behind the desk, as if to kill time during a predictable response. Soon after, Cal cupped his hands behind his head and released a howl of bewilderment.

"When you're ready to die, you're ready to serve," the man said. "This is a training facility. We run operations that exist far beyond the fold. That man you saw ripped apart for months? He's now hunting pirates in the Scarabbi Cluster."

"You mean to tell me," Cal said, "that I could have walked out of here anytime I wanted?"

"Yes."

Cal shook his head. "13 years. I spent 13 years here."

"You spent 13 years in training."

"Some spent less than one."

"And they all died."

Cal flinched.

"Don't get me wrong," the man said. "The reckless are useful too. We are more than happy to grant the death wishes of any who seek it. I can't recall a single 'fodder-type' who lasted more than a year after Descent." He fanned his fingers, then pointed at Cal. "You, on the other hand, are the kind of trainee that holds significantly more value. After 13 years in a box, you came to see death as an opportunity. So what difference does it make if the freedom you sought was earned or given?"

Cal glared at the man. "And what if I refuse?"

"Then you die."

The matter-of-fact response caught Cal off-guard. "That's it?"

"In agreeing to Descent, you were ready to die. We are not going to be so heartless as to deny you that opportunity. Just say the word and we can do it right now. Quick and painless."

Cal glanced around the room without moving his head.

"Or," the man continued, "you can live a new life as a secret operative."

"Doing what?"

"Wherever we deem necessary."

Cal scoffed and glanced away.

The man smiled and softened his tone. "I can assure you this. You will leave this facility intact and unharmed. You will be fed, clothed, housed, and given your freedom, as promised."

"But."

"But when we call, you answer. There will not be a second incarceration."

Cal lowered his head and thought for a moment. "So I can die here and now, or I can die as a pawn out in the black."

"Many operatives live long and happy lives after Descent."

Cal chuckled. "And how many of them die of old age?"

The man smirked, then shrugged. "Your choice."

*   *   *

Seven years later, Cal was enjoying a quiet dinner inside the kitchen of a small house. It wasn't much in terms of spatial living, but compared to the prison cell, it was a mansion. Heather, his longtime partner, reached across the small table with her fork and stabbed a morsel from his plate. They chuckled as a brief game of fork-swords saw Heather snatch victory. Their playful smiles mirrored each other, highlighting a deep contentment that filled the abode.

The cottage rested atop a hill that overlooked a lush valley. As one of a few dozen homes along the hillside, it represented a significant chunk of the population. That particular outpost served as a base of operations for a new asteroid belt, one with a high concentration of precious minerals. The colony was established after terraforming the largest rock inside the belt, essentially a small moon. What started as a lawless experiment had blossomed into a tight-knit community. Cal was a thriving member, serving as both councilman and security officer.

A knock at the door caught the couple's attention.

"I got it," Cal said, tossing his napkin onto the table.

"A little late for Kira rounds," Heather said.

"I know, right?" He stood up and made his way to the door. "Should I invite her in for a bite?"

"Sure, we got plenty to go around."

Cal nodded, then opened the door to an unfamiliar face in a

three-piece suit. The whole concept of unfamiliarity was a bit surprising, given the size of the colony. Perhaps a visit from the managing body, but even they sent notice beforehand. "Can I help you?" he said to the mystery man.

"Been a while, Mr. McCready."

The voice conjured a distant memory.

Cal's face morphed from curiosity to concern. He glanced back at Heather, who read the message loud and clear. She excused herself without a word and retreated to the bedroom, leaving the unfinished meal on the table. The bedroom door whined shut and a soft rustle filled the background. Cal returned his gaze to the man, still standing on the sill.

"May I come inside?"

"You grew a beard."

The man shrugged.

Cal reached forward and poked the man's chest.

The man cocked an eyebrow.

"Just checking," Cal said, then stepped aside.

The man entered the domicile and glanced into a small living room. Lounge chairs, side tables with lamps, bookshelves, the hallmarks of simple living. He continued into the modest kitchen and took a seat in Cal's chair. Cal sneered and claimed the other, still warm from Heather's presence. The man tossed one leg over the other and rested an elbow on the table. Cal crossed his arms atop the table and stared the man down, primed yet impatient.

"Wondered when you'd show up," Cal said.

"Not pleased to see me?"

"Not pleased with the circumstance."

"Still bitter, I see."

"Hard not to be when you're wrongfully imprisoned."

The man smirked. "Is that what we did?"

Cal cringed and leaned back in the chair. The metal legs creaked atop the floor, needling the schism between the two men. Cal maintained his guarded demeanor. His eyes burrowed into his opponent, as if goading him to draw first.

"You killed three people in self-defense," the man said plainly. "That was never in doubt. And yes, one of them was somewhat important. But, given your state at the time, both physically and mentally, have you ever wondered where you would have ended up by now?"

Cal softened a bit.

The man glanced around the clean and cozy kitchen, then down to the half-eaten meal between them. The morsels were still steaming after a thoughtful preparation. "Seems like you're doing quite well."

"Could have done well regardless."

The man leaned closer. "Cal, you weren't some misguided kid on the street. You were a decorated soldier. Trained, cunning, lethal. And you were in a bad spot after the war. You might say that your little incident was a blessing in disguise."

"So you helped me by sending me to prison."

"We sent you to a place where you could help yourself. Your skills and experience gave you tremendous value. You just needed some time to reset."

Cal shifted his gaze to a nearby window. The lush valley gained a sudden clarity.

"Ask yourself," the man said. "Who are the most qualified peacekeepers? Missionaries? Their agendas alienate people. Military? Corporations? Same problem. No, the best peacekeeper is the average Joe. Someone with skin in the game. A local leader with fortitude and conviction. *That* person can have a long and lasting impact on the lives around them."

Cal rapped his fingers on the table, unable to retort.

"You, Cal McCready, have made this outpost a better place. It's safe, secure, and productive. *Your* freedom became *their* freedom."

The statement hit Cal harder than expected. His gaze fell and he nodded slowly, taking stock of the hard work and dedication over the last several years.

"So your mission," the man said with due respect, "is to stay here and die of old age."

Cal smiled at the half-eaten meal, then glanced at the bedroom door, where Heather was dutifully planning their assumed exit. *What a reveal this will be*, he thought. The burden of anticipation departed his shoulders. His posture slumped and a heavy sigh escaped his chest.

"Though you did try to murder me," the man said with a mocking tone.

Cal rolled his eyes.

"Buuut, I guess we can let that slide." The man slapped the table, then stood from the chair and straightened his suit. "And on that note, I should bid you a fond farewell."

Cal rose to his feet. "So that's it then?"

"That's it. Just keep on keepin' on." The man smiled and offered his hand.

"I will," Cal said and completed the shake.

The man turned to leave, but Cal did not release his grip. His hand tightened, forcing the man to stumble back and regain eye contact. Cal stared him down as decades of resentment coursed through his body. The man responded with annoyance, which quickly turned to anger.

A tense standoff commenced.

"Let go of my hand, Cal," the man said sternly.

"Here's the thing," Cal said, refusing to budge. "You locked me up under the guise of saving my life. You locked me up to serve the greater good. And maybe you did." With the other hand, Cal reached into his rear waistband, retrieved a plasma pistol, and lowered it to his side. He leaned forward, bringing them face-to-face. "But that wasn't your decision to make."

"You're still bio-locked, Cal," the man said, slightly rattled. "You can't kill me."

"No." Cal smiled, then gestured to the side. "But she can."

The man turned into the barrel of another plasma pistol. Heather pulled the trigger, sending a bolt of white-hot energy through the man's forehead. It tore through his skull, painting the wall behind him with blood and brains. Cal released his grip as the headless body crumpled to the floor. He snatched a napkin from the table and wiped the blood splatter from his face.

"That's a shame," he said, tossing the napkin aside. "I really liked this place."

"Me too," Heather said. She smiled, then turned for the front door.

They grabbed the go-bags from outside the bedroom and disappeared into the night.

THE END

Betrayal is the deadliest of games.

Burke is a member of the Mako Brotherhood, one of the most notorious criminal gangs in the galaxy. He is summoned to a secret haven for an important mission, but the sect is unaware that his loyalty has been brutally compromised.

BANDOLIER

The moon's atmosphere was more chaotic than usual, not that the pilot cared. His ship was more than capable and his racing mind was searching for any distraction. Acidic rain peppered the viewport as he guided the stealth fighter through a thick and menacing haze. Lightning bolts flashed through the clouds. His grip tightened on the yoke as he fought to steady his nerves. The haze parted after a brief descent, revealing a hellscape of jagged rock.

And so it began.

The ship, a dark and slender craft with a knife-like edge, was designed to slice through any climate with ease. Its twin ionic engines were encased in blast shielding that dampened sound and light. Most of its victims never saw it coming. And on this particular approach, it was an advantage that the pilot sorely wished to leverage.

But the cannons remained cold.

For the moment, the fighter was a simple shuttle.

A dull blue light appeared in the distance. It was nestled at the base of two large mountains and hovered atop a sheet of fog. The light pulsed ever so slightly, like a demonic eye beckoning its prey. The man loosened his grip and took a deep breath, anticipating the crackle of static that followed.

"Kizzek voch un mesha," said a robotic voice through the intercom.

"Nora hosh enuka," the man said quickly, lest he face a barrage of interceptor missiles.

The intercom crackled away.

And that was that.

Voice scan confirmed.

Access code confirmed.

He knew this because he was still breathing. Nobody visited the Mako Brotherhood on a whim. At least, not without immediately meeting one's maker. The man, on the other hand, was an esteemed member. Nevertheless, every approach needed verification, no matter what remote world the criminal sect currently occupied.

As he neared the refuge, the dull reflection of a landing pad came into view. The digital camouflage was deactivated, leaving a smooth platform of tarnished metal. It rose slightly to provide a visual separation. The ship glided to a stop and pressed its landing gear to the surface. Thrusters spun down and the platform restored its cloak, merging the ship into the mountain. The sharp hull blended seamlessly into the craggy facade.

The man sat motionless inside the cockpit.

No welcome message.

No guided instructions.

Just the cold silence of clearance.

He closed his eyes, released a heavy sigh, then unbuckled from the pilot seat and made his way to the cargo bay. The space was small and limited, being a fighter ship. It got the job done, but longer missions required regular restocks. He stepped over a few crates and settled at the airlock door. A simple satchel was hanging from a nearby wall hook. He snatched the bag, tossed it over his shoulder, then tapped the control panel beside the door. It slid open, inviting a rush of humid air into the bay. The man filled his lungs with the familiar scents of musk and mold. As hideouts went, it was very effective at repulsing the senses.

He leapt from the craft and landed on the metal plane with a heavy thump. A steady drizzle pecked at his skin and clothes. Droplets rolled off the sturdy leather and fell to the ground. The garb was designed for such conditions and had served the man well. Thick boots provided more than enough support as he stepped across the slippery rock towards the glowing blue entrance. A pair of plasma pistols clung to his vest, one across the chest and one across the belly. Freedom of motion was vital out in the black, as danger came from all directions.

The blue light brightened as the man neared. What began as a distant port had grown into a mighty entry several meters tall. As he passed through the frame, his steps morphed from wet clomps to harsh clanks. An armored door slid shut, cloaking him in darkness.

And with darkness came dread.

Soon after, a wash of sterile light filled the corridor. The passage was long and narrow, yet reasonably spacious. Numerous wires and conduits snaked overhead. They were bound to the ceiling in random bundles, giving the tunnel a transient aura. Puffs of steam rose through the slotted floor. A lighting panel flickered in the distance. The space needled the man's calm. And for a moment, he welcomed a return to the dark.

He gathered his wits, then continued forward with a resolute stride. Heavy plods echoed through the tunnel like a drill sergeant on his way to crack some skulls. As he neared the end, a pair of flanking alcoves revealed themselves. Two heavily armed guards stepped into the corridor to meet the visitor. Body armor encased them from head to toe, like sentinels prepped for battle. The man maintained his stride, unfazed by the sudden threat. The guards nodded as he passed, having never touched their weapons. The man returned the nod. No stop, no frisk, just an unspoken certitude.

He was a member, after all.

And membership had its privileges.

Critical, invaluable privileges.

The man rounded a corner at the end of the passage and entered a modest mess hall. A dozen Brotherhood members sat around a handful of tables and chairs. Several cubbies lined the walls, containing everything from food stocks to clothing. The area served as a multi-use chamber where members relaxed for meals, traded goods, and gathered for missions.

Conversations quieted as the man appeared. He smiled and nodded at various cohorts as he marched through the space. They responded by tapping their chests, signaling respect for rank. The man passed through the room and turned down another hallway, allowing the mess hall to return to its usual chatter.

After a brief walk, the man stopped at a series of bio-locked doors. Scan plates glowed red with restricted access. The rooms were used for anything of high value, be it precious cargo or secret meetings.

The latter was his purpose for this particular day.

He stepped to the appropriate door and paused for a mental reset. The weight upon his mind grew heavier. He hiked up his sleeve to reveal a control device that wrapped around his forearm. A few taps powered the device and confirmed its activation. His racing mind studied the screen as if seeing it for the first time. Panic began to bubble inside his throat. His eyes closed. A wave of concentration consumed him, relaxing muscles and slowing breaths. The panic subsided. He opened his eyes, rolled down the sleeve, and pressed his palm to the scanner.

The plate pinged and turned green.

The door unlatched and slid open.

He stepped forward into a dimly lit room where three men sat at a central table. Ribbons of cigar smoke lifted from a pair of crystal ashtrays. Several bottles littered the grimy surface. The space was cramped, but with enough room to wander around the table. The men were playing cards and bantering about the latest missions. Two were dressed in mercenary garb. One wore a more commanding ensemble, and his rank among the men was obvious to a fault. They all turned to greet the visitor.

"Burke," said the leader in a graveled voice. "Just in time. Have a seat." He pointed to the empty chair with a cigar in hand.

"Gentlemen," Burke said as he claimed his seat.

"How was the trip?" another man said.

"Fine. A bit chaotic on approach, but the ship managed okay."

"Those storm cells have been an absolute nightmare," the leader said. "My haulers have been grounded for six days."

The next game started, which included Burke. He glanced down at a small pile of cards forming beside a fresh glass of bourbon. It was the good stuff, too. Kiwaskan Province. They took good care of him. He took a sip and grunt-nodded, savoring the moment.

"*Six days*, Burke," the leader said.

Burke sighed. "Which is why I'm here."

"Precisely," the other man said. "We can overload three haulers, but we only have two competent pilots. I know it ain't the most glamourous job, but—"

"I get it," Burke said. He nodded slowly while staring into his glass. "There's only one problem."

The leader shrugged and motioned to continue.

Burke paused to summon the courage. "There isn't going to be a job." His eyes locked onto the leader, whose sympathetic gaze scrunched with confusion. "Or any job. Ever again." Burke reached into a side pocket and withdrew a small puck-like device. The oval shape and dull red glow were instantly recognizable to everyone present.

A bomb.

This particular bomb was favored by bounty hunters. It created a bio-link with the owner, turning them into a walking weapon. The bomb was triggered on command, or if the owner died, making it the ultimate arbitrator in a high-stakes negotiation. But to use one in this context, within the walls of the Brotherhood, was the highest form of treason. Burke knew that. But it didn't matter. He lowered the device to the table and slid it to the center.

The other two men could only gawk in disbelief as a sudden dread infected their bodies. To make sense of this action would be to understand the deepest of sorrows, the darkest of faculties, the follies of all broken men. They were frozen, helpless, slaves to anticipation.

The leader, on the other hand, ignored the device. His eyes remained on Burke. The glassy orbs were soft and contemplative, like a disappointed father.

"Who got to you?" the leader said.

"Doesn't matter," Burke said.

"It does to me."

Burke sighed and lowered his gaze. A biting silence infected the room. Seconds ticked with the might of a sledgehammer. The very concept of betrayal was as foreign as breathing water. And yet, there they were, staring into the great unknown as a fractured family. Burke reached across his chest and withdrew a plasma pistol. As tears pooled beneath his eyes, he turned to one of the men and lifted the weapon.

The man, also tearful, met his gaze.

"I love you, brother," Burke said, then pulled the trigger.

A white-hot bolt tore through the man's skull and splattered its contents across the rear wall. Blood and brains crept down the pane as the headless body slumped forward onto the table. The grisly stump oozed blood across the felted surface.

The other man raised his hands, begging for reprieve. "Wait. Please, wait."

"Thank you for the kindness, brother," Burke said, then pulled the trigger again.

Another flash, another splatter, another illusion shattered.

Burke turned the pistol to the leader as tears rolled down his cheeks. The leader hadn't flinched, hadn't groveled, hadn't reacted in any way. Instead, he maintained an uncorrupted affection for his brother-in-arms.

"Who?" the leader said, his eyes glistening.

"You'll meet him shortly," Burke said, then flipped a switch on his weapon and fired again. But instead of a plasma bolt, a shock round hammered the leader's chest. His body jostled inside a static surge, then fell limp in the chair. Burke reached over and gripped the man's shoulder. "I had no choice," he said as the leader slipped into a dreamless oblivion.

Burke sobbed.

A torrent of loss and regret flooded his mind. Tears rained onto the table. The necessity was clear, but the reality was cruel and unrelenting. He wept openly as his psyche was torn to shreds. And yet, the path to salvation had only just begun.

There was work to do.

With a final heave, the mourning turned to motivation. He wiped his face clean and stood from the chair, careful to avoid the grisly puddles creeping around the room. A singular focus consumed him. He removed his satchel and dumped its contents on the table. Body bag, tape, rope, everything he needed for the task at hand. He hooked the unconscious leader by the armpits and laid him flat on the floor.

The work was swift.

Mouth taped.

Limbs bound.

Body bagged.

Before long, the package was ready for delivery.

Burke contemplated the most efficient exit. The escape tunnels were too narrow and craggy. Certain capture. A shootout with a dozen mercenaries was reckless at best. Certain death. He needed a distraction. Or at the very least, fewer targets. He eyed the puck-bomb still resting on the table. And with a grunt of realization, the plan was set.

Burke swiped the device and tucked it into a satchel pocket. He added some random items to the main compartment and tossed the bag over his shoulder. A final scan of the carnage evoked little emotion. The sorrow would be tremendous, but it would have to wait. The mission was in motion. "Rest well, brothers," he said to the departed, then grabbed the rope around the leader's feet and dragged him out of the room.

Back inside the hallway, Burke parked the package against the wall and gently closed the door. He used the brighter light inside the tunnel for a quick self-assessment. No obvious blood, just a small splatter on a dark shirt. Not a concern. He wiped his face and raked his hair. No red. He could smell the char from the plasma strikes.

Cigar smoke for all they knew.

Good to go.

He reclaimed an air of calm and stepped towards the mess hall, leaving the body out of sight. Soundproof chambers meant that the roar of conversation had continued through the slaughter. Privacy was paramount inside the dens of disrepute. The secrets they contained were invaluable, and their protection came at the ultimate cost.

Burke rounded a corner, bringing the mess hall into view. He maintained a confident pace, conveying the poise and composure of rank. His heavy plods caught several eyes. More heads turned as he entered the room, dulling the discourse. The vibe was stern yet civil, and Burke was determined to keep it that way. With a final step, he halted at the center of the room and claimed the space with a loud clap.

"Attention, brothers," he said with a commanding voice.

The chatter ceased.

All eyes turned to the lieutenant.

"I have an important announcement to make. If you would be so kind, please join me here in the center. It won't take long, then you can get back to whatever bullshit I stole you from."

A few chuckles responded and the majority rose to their feet. One table stubbornly refused, where three mercenaries traded wary glances.

Reading the room, Burke quickly pivoted to regain trust. "Don't worry," he said to the resistant group. "This is straight from the top. I don't think it warrants a song and dance, but I don't get to make that decision. Just humor me for a minute." He added a shrug, then turned his attention to the gathering mass.

One member sighed, then nodded to the others. All three rose and joined the circle. With everyone assembled, Burke twisted around the center while exchanging pleasantries. He sighed mockingly, then addressed the group. "Thank you, brothers. And I must apologize ahead of time because this will be kind of dumb."

More chuckles.

"So without further ado, let's get this over with." Burke removed his satchel, then slowly scanned the group to select the most agreeable person he could find. And find him he did. "Brother Fillian, if you would be so kind." He extended the satchel and invited the young man into the circle.

Fillian stepped forward and grasped the satchel. Burke smiled, then leaned forward and whispered some instructions into his ear. The men eyed each other with mild concern, which Burke deftly stifled with a chipper grin.

"You're gonna love this," he said, then exited the circle and stepped towards the nearest table. Once behind, he turned to face the group. As he gripped the table edge, the mounting unease reached a breaking point.

Smiles faded.

Dread descended.

"I am truly sorry," Burke said with a somber tone, then flipped the table forward. Chairs scraped across the floor as he ducked behind the toppled pane. The group began to scatter, but it was too late. "Bandolier," he said, triggering the bomb.

The explosion ripped through the bodies of all twelve mercenaries. Heads and limbs were torn from torsos and scattered through the room. The fireball slammed into the fallen table and shoved Burke backwards several feet. The heat was immense, but he remained intact. Debris bounced around the space and clattered to a rest. Tables were toppled, chairs were mangled, cubbies were painted with gore.

And much to Burke's horror, a lone voice cried in agony. Someone had survived, and was badly wounded. Heavy tromps echoed from the opposite tunnel. The guards were on their way, as expected. Mercy would have to wait.

Burke stood from behind the table and quickly surveyed the aftermath. Blood was splattered in a perfect circle, creating a gruesome flower. Its petals slithered through the carnage and back to the charred center. Fillian was vaporized, but the others were violently dismembered. There was one survivor. The man was battered and brutalized, using an elbow stump to pull himself to an illusion of safety. Burke swallowed the guilt and sprinted towards the exit tunnel. He skidded to a halt beside the port and pressed his back to the wall inside the mess hall. Instinct pulled his hands to the plasma pistols. He snatched them from their holsters and held them aloft.

The guards drew closer.

Burke held his breath.

The armored pair sprinted by and stumbled to a stop.

Their weapons were drawn, but the ghastly sight derailed the call of duty. Carnage on the battlefield was expected, but home was sacred. The violation of sanctuary was enough to stun any man. It was the moment Burke had counted on. He lunged forward with both pistols raised and fired bolts into the backs of their necks. As a senior member, he knew the armor as well as they did. He knew the strengths. He also knew the weak points. And with two skillfully placed shots, he severed their spines and dropped their lifeless bodies to the floor.

Burke emptied his lungs, then hurried over to the sole survivor. The man, still scraping the floor with an exposed bone, heard the approach and turned to meet his fate. Half of his face was burned, but he met Burke's gaze with one good eye. Once an exchange of respect, now a pained question. Burke had no answer. Without a word, he raised his weapon and ended the misery.

The blast echoed through the facility, then faded into a grim silence. Burke stared at the corpse beneath the smoking muzzle. A lifeless eye stared back at him, peering into the world beyond worlds. It was a snapshot in time, a moment scorched into memory. Burke could only absorb the reality in cold silence.

No forgetting.

No turning back.

Only forward.

He returned the weapons to the holsters and stepped through the horrifying aftermath. A grisly soup squished beneath his feet as he returned to the hallway, where the dormant body of the leader rested in wait. Red footprints followed him down the passage. He rounded a corner, grabbed the rope, and resumed his trek towards the exit. The body was heavy, but it gained a lightness as it slid through the bloody muck. Burke maintained a steady pace. He shuttered his mind and locked his eyes forward. But as he passed the two guards, the pretense was lost. He released his grip and turned to face the massacre.

"It wasn't supposed to be this way!" he said, wearing his pain for none to see. The shout echoed through the mess hall and down the tunnels. Anger swelled inside his chest. His furious gaze dropped to the body bag and he kicked the leader with all his might. "*You* did this! *You* did! It's *your* fault, you son of a bitch!" More kicks followed, warping the bag with every blow. He reared back for another strike, but stopped.

The rage quieted.

An image had captured his mind, breaking through the madness and restoring control. He reached down, grabbed the rope, and resumed the departure.

* * *

Several hours and a hyperjump later, Burke and his stealth fighter punched through the atmosphere of another remote world. The passenger in the cargo bay remained limp and lifeless. The body bag was latched to the floor like any other piece of freight. Despite the calmness of transport, a frightful anticipation had consumed the ship. The cockpit was eerily tranquil, as if destiny itself was along for the ride.

Burke scanned a vast and open landscape that offered little to the eye. Rolling hills, once rich in minerals, were mined dry and abandoned. Rusted rails snaked across the plains and into the yawning mouths of tunnels. Every portal was reclaimed by dust and vermin. Refining facilities dotted the landscape, their rotting shells long forgotten.

One such facility pinged on a hologram map, catching Burke's attention. He had received the coordinates after departing the stronghold. Phase one completed, phase two commenced. As the ship neared the facility, a detailed layout appeared beside the map. Burke studied the image and selected a landing spot. Soon after, the ship touched down inside an old receiving yard.

Burke powered down the console and proceeded to the airlock. The door slid open and he dropped to the cracked pavement. After a brief scan of the area, he turned to fetch the package. He unlatched the bag, hoisted it onto his shoulders, and trotted towards the facility. A clear and singular focus commanded every step.

The end was near, and salvation beckoned his arrival.

He glanced up at the rusted refinery. Two stories of warped metal rose from the sandy ground. Cranes and conveyors reached into the open air like a giant spider. Chains dangled from the arms and clattered in the wind. Several loading bays lined the bottom floor, one of which was open. Burke refocused on the entry and continued forward.

He passed under the frame and into a dusty hellscape. Sullied machinery filled the interior, long past their salvageability. Holes in the metal roof cast beams of light onto the grimy floor. Numerous chemical stains created a toxic mosaic. The remaining space was cloaked in darkness, hiding its secrets from the outside world.

As Burke neared the center, a slight glimmer caught his eye.

There, trapped in a sunbeam, was a pair of shackles chained to a floor drain.

As expected.

Burke took a deep breath and pushed towards the finish line. His careful steps echoed through the cavernous interior. He paused a few meters before the drain and gently lowered his package to the floor. Now physically unburdened, he craved the mental freedom as well. He took his final steps, dropped to his knees, and grabbed the open shackle. Without hesitation, he placed a wrist into the cuff and locked himself to the drain.

Mission complete.

The exertion left him breathless. His lungs swelled and deflated as his eyes surveyed the darkness. An ominous presence lurked in the shadows. It haunted him from afar, circling his mind like a hungry predator.

One minute became two.

Two became three.

And four became unbearable.

"I did it!" he screamed, his words echoing through the facility. "It's done!" His manic gaze darted around the room. "Where is he?! Where is my boy?!"

Footsteps crept through the darkness.

Burke whipped his gaze to the source as a shadowy figure emerged from the abyss. Black leather encased it from neck to toe. A cloth hood concealed its face. A man, an apparition, Burke could not tell. He could only gawk at the figure like a lost child.

"Where is he?!" Burke said again. "You stole him! You stole him from me! You're a coward and a monster!" He panted through the rage, then swallowed the outburst and fought to slow his breathing. Calmness returned, and with it, a plea for absolution. "I did what you asked. I did it. Please. Please give me back my boy."

The figure stepped around the floor drain, staying just out of reach. It halted at the package, then leaned down for an inspection. A quick unzip revealed the prize, the infamous leader of the Mako Brotherhood. In the flesh, alive and breathing. The figure glanced at Burke, then rezipped the bag and returned to its feet.

"Please," Burke said as tears rolled down his cheeks.

The figure loomed over him in silent contemplation.

"Please," Burke said again, clasping his hands.

In a single fluid motion, the figure unlatched a pistol from its belt and shot Burke in the chest. The shock round jostled his frame and dropped him to the floor in a crumpled heap. As he lay there, stunned and battered, the figure stepped forward and knelt beside him. It placed a hand on his shoulder as the world slipped away.

* * *

Several hours later, Burke awoke on the same grimy floor. The pain of impact was still radiating inside his chest, and the wooziness of shock was slow to fade. But something was different. His hand was free. The dark figure was gone. And in its place, a furry creature was desperately trying to rouse him.

Burke's eyes popped open as a rush of joy enveloped his body.

A small dog was furiously licking his face.

"Bandy!" Burke said, then scrambled to his knees and scooped the mutt into his arms. The licking continued as he swayed back and forth. He hugged the dog tightly, like a life raft in open water. "Bandy! Oh Bandy! My sweet Bandolier!"

* * *

The next day, two agents were sitting inside an interrogation room. They occupied one side of a table and stared at a man on the other side. This man, one of the Federation's most wanted, was deemed uncatchable. Yet there he was, the head of the serpent. The leader of the Mako Brotherhood stared back at them with limbs chained to the floor. His face was bruised, but his demeanor was oddly receptive. He didn't expect to be there any more than the agents did. And when miracles happen, they tend to open the mind.

The simple concrete room was a few meters wide with a door on one side and a one-way mirror on the other. Behind the mirror were two more agents. One wore a face of utter disbelief, as if watching a ghost divulge its secrets. She leaned forward and huffed with pure intrigue. The other looked on with a neutral expression. His arms were crossed. He stood firm and still, as if suffering through a boring movie.

"How did you do it?" the woman said.

"Kidnapped a lieutenant's family," the man said bluntly.

"Impossible. Members of the Brotherhood don't have families."

"This one did."

"Bullshit." She turned a skeptical gaze to the man. "Mako was founded on the premise that you can't pressure an outcast. Band over blood. That's their entire thing. They're a roaming gang of orphans."

The man paused for thought, then turned to meet her gaze. "How's Peaches doing?"

"My cat? What the hell does that—"

"Do you love him?"

"Very much so."

"Would you consider him part of the family?"

"Well, yes, but—"

"You also have a daughter. And a husband. Your parents are still alive and you are an active presence in their lives. Family is what keeps us grounded. You are tethered to the bedrock of the human condition." He turned back to the interrogation. "The Mako Brotherhood tried to replicate that. But in creating a facsimile, they made one critical error."

The woman grunted with understanding. "They failed to define family."

"Unconditional love, regardless of species, is a tonic more powerful than any drug."

"So you kidnapped his dog."

The man nodded. "He murdered sixteen militants to get it back, and then hand-delivered one of the most notorious criminals in the galaxy."

"Clever," the woman said. "Abhorrent, but clever."

"Just pulling an unseen lever."

"So what I'm hearing is, if I ever want you to do anything for me, all I need to do is swipe your poodle."

The man shrugged. "Only if you want to be skinned alive and fed to the vultures."

They shared a wary chuckle, then resumed the watch in silence.

THE END

A foolish choice leads to a fateful trap.

After a night on the town, Nate is hungover and sick as a dog. He is also late for a cosmic cruise and nearly misses the launch. As he settles in for an epic voyage, his dream vacation is slowly revealed as a deadly snare.

STARSHIP ETERNITY

I'm fairly certain I need to vomit again. That's the only thought my brain can muster while staring at the sweaty monster in the bathroom mirror. The previous night remains a blur. I remember the club, the music, the dancing, the absurd amount of booze, everything up to the room spinning out of control. Quite frankly, it's nothing short of a miracle that I made it back to the hotel. I can't recall a single step, let alone what got me to—

And there it is.

Right in the sink.

Disgusting.

Anyway, I guess I shouldn't expect much from a raging hangover. Throbbing headache, foggy memory, a deep sense of self-loathing. But hey, I'm in one piece and my luggage is intact. That's a win. In retrospect, I shouldn't have started the party before I got to the cruise ship. And now I have to trek three blocks to the spaceport. Three fucking blocks in this condition. Maybe it's time for a little hair of the dog. But what? Beer? Wine? Perhaps a little—

Nope.

Gross.

I should leave a big tip for housekeeping.

Okay then, just gonna muscle through it. I can do three blocks. My bags are packed, I look like death, and it's time for a long vacation. But first, I need to utter those four familiar words. I always say them after an evening bender. It's practically a tradition at this point.

"I should stop drinking."

There. Who knows, maybe they'll stick this time. Unlikely, given that I bought a drink pass. An open bar for an entire month? Jeez, that's dangerous. But you only live once, right? It's time to chug my way across the galaxy. Maybe I'll start with a—

Ugh.

* * *

Chaotic city streets are not the best tonic for a hangover. It's a relentless assault from every direction. Car horns bash my brain like baseball bats. At least the shuttle buses are kind enough to hum quietly overhead. I would take one if I weren't so late already. I can thank the checkout desk for that one. As it turns out, arguing about room charges is nigh impossible when your liver is still struggling to purge the previous evening. The receptionist was totally out of line with her impatient translating of my mumbled jargon.

Okay, yeah, I'm the asshole.

And now I have to cover three blocks in 20 minutes.

Backpack? Check.

Rolling suitcase? Check.

Breath so bad it could kill a pigeon? Check.

Eternity Cruises, here I come!

Thankfully, I travel light, even for a month-long vacation. One of the best pieces of advice I ever received came from a business tycoon at a spaceport bar. "Want to have a better vacation?" she said after I tried and failed to hit on her. "Unpack half your luggage and bring more money." That nugget comes in quite handy when a sickly sprint lies between you and your departure.

I take a deep breath, then start running.

It goes fine for the first half-block, but then my very-out-of-shape lungs make it abundantly clear that running is not an approved activity. I wheeze to a stop, swallow a vomit, catch what little breath I have, resume a fast walk, then struggle back to sprint. A quarter block later, rinse and repeat. People sneer at me with a mixture of pity and disgust. I swallow it all because I don't have time to unpack my insecurities in public.

For the record, I hate Marcoza. Always have. It's a crap city in a crap location on a crap planet. The only redeeming feature is that you're largely free to do what you want, so long as you don't interfere with the daily flow. Party on, just don't get in the way. Unfortunately, that attracts a certain type of folk. I admire the "live and let live" attitude, but this place pushes that mantra to the absolute limit.

Why am I saying this? Because no one has shown me an ounce of respect. Yes, I'm out of shape. Yes, I'm blocking foot traffic. Just grumble your curses and go around. But no, that's too civilized. Instead, I receive three shoulder knocks and a shin kick. That's *four* confirmations of *me* being the asshole. Technically five, counting the receptionist. I'm not looking for help, just an old geezer to say, "Wish I could run like that."

Okay, enough bellyaching.

Just get to the damn ship.

Sprint, wheeze, stop, cough.

Sprint, wheeze, stop, cough.

Sprint, wheeze, stop, cough.

Aaaaaand, disco.

The spaceport is as ugly as I remember. Rusty cranes, broken pavement, a lingering aroma of salty farts. Damp garbage overflows from neglected dumpsters. The entire area is gray and painfully uninviting. It butts up against a heavily polluted bay where ships hover above the water in idle wait. No launchpads here, that would be too costly (read: safe). It's cheaper to taxi out into open water and launch from there. And on the off chance that a ship fails, a gentle splashdown means less repair time. The tradeoff is a steady mist of sewage water, hence the smell.

The hyper-bland terminal is a series of concrete boxes with black windows. It looks like a sketch by a child who was told to draw buildings. Squares inside squares. Perfect.

A small army of hucksters crowd the entry, badgering tourists to buy whatever "authentic" garbage they are selling this week. They surround every taxi and get shooed away like flies. It's like the industry deliberately chose the most offensive launch location in the galaxy. But given the city, it doesn't take an economist to see how much money they save (and regulations they avoid) by using the port equivalent of a gypsy campground. Somewhere in the muck, a sack of cash is being handed to a greasy politician.

Ah well, it won't matter in a few minutes. I'll be at the bar, watching the port windows turn from blue to black. But first things first, let's get to the damn ship.

I shove my way through a sea of junk peddlers, hurling curses loudly and freely, which earns me a random jab to the kidney. So I refuse to buy your trash and I'm the asshole? Again? I swear, this day can't end fast enough. I swallow the urge to bicker and finally arrive at the gate. Two guards greet my arrival. One of them looks me up and down, then cringes. Sweet mercy, I just ran three blocks with a boss-level hangover. Fuck you and your silly little uniform.

"Starship Eternity?" he says to me.

"Eternity, yeah," I say. His assumption catches me off guard and I soften my desire to snap back. I simply flash my comdev ticket, show my passport, and they wave me through without a frisk or tickle. That's some lax-ass security if you ask me. Whatever. I made it.

"Last line on the left," the other guard says, then points me in the direction.

"Thanks," I say with a hint of derision.

Unpleasant, but efficient. I'm okay with that.

I join the line in question and release a heavy sigh. The lady in front of me turns to say hello. She's an older woman with frizzy white hair bound in a loose ponytail. No makeup, no dress, just simple duds with a small travel case and a no-fucks-given attitude. Respect.

"Hello there," she says with a confident voice.

"Hi," I say back.

"Ready for the grand departure?"

"Whatever gets me off this rock."

She chuckles, then extends her hand. "Abigale."

I complete the shake. "Nathan, but you can call me Nate."

"A pleasure to meet you, Nate."

"You as well."

She smiles wide and nods. "I'll be at the Sundial Lounge for takeoff if you want to tie one on with me."

I crack a smile. "Abby, are you hitting on me?"

"Yes."

The matter-of-fact response causes me to stammer. I struggle to find any words, given how utterly unprepared I am for such an encounter. An open invitation from grandma was not how I envisioned my vacation starting. I can only muster an awkward chuckle.

"Think about it," she says, then turns to rejoin the line.

"I will," I say, then glance over my shoulder to find some sympathy.

The man behind me, a gaunt fellow with sun-wrecked skin, gives me a smirk and shrug. *I'd hit it*, he says with his eyes.

I can only nod because my brain refuses to accept that this is a real exchange. I return to my forward-facing position and go about minding my own damn business. Ooo, look, a crack in the pavement. I shall give it my undivided attention.

After a few minutes of shuffling forward, I reach the gangway and another set of guards. They are dressed in white, oddly enough. A poor choice of wardrobe in this hellscape. Their dry cleaning bills must be staggering. No weapons, no gear, not even a commanding hat. Whatever. It's the last checkpoint before I can dump my shit and get on with the trip. I offer my ticket, but they are strangely disinterested. Instead, one of the guards lifts a scanner and points it at me.

"Stand still," she says.

I was standing still. Okay, so I stand stiller.

A laser dot appears on my forehead and she squeezes the trigger. The device pings and displays a panel of data. Bio-sig? Health check?

Fuck if I know. She studies it for a moment, then scrunches her brow and consults her colleague.

"Hmm," the other guard says, clearly confused.

"What is this?" I say.

They ignore me. This day, I swear.

The man pokes at the device, then shrugs. He looks at me, then at the other guard, then back at me. "I mean, look at him."

"Look at me what?"

"Yeah," she says, then waves me through.

Seriously, what the hell? I can only huff and continue forward. I step onto a metal gangway, officially departing solid land for the next month. The grated panels give me a lovely view of the garbage water several meters below. Thank goodness for the sturdy railing. Anyone falling into that filth would need to shower for a week.

I glance down the shoreline where several other ships hover in wait. A few are also boarding, but my last-minute arrival means that we'll be leaving first. And given the port of departure, I only recognize about half the companies. There are always some new names, as the cruising industry is notorious for fly-by-night retrofits. I once saw a converted ice hauler. That's like painting a dump truck and calling it a limousine. I do see another ship from Eternity Cruises, so they must be doing well. A small comfort at this particular port.

My ship is a multi-deck luxury liner with a vibrant flare. At least, that's what the brochure said. This one looks more like an oversized transport shuttle with an allergy to color. As I near the end of the gangway, my eyes narrow as I survey a stark white exterior dotted with window ports. Maybe I'm still too hungover to process pigmentation. In any case, it looks like someone dunked the entire ship in a bucket of bleach. Ah well, at least the size is right.

The gangway ends at a wide airlock. Passengers step into the right side while pallets of supplies hover into the left. A team of robots tends to the pallets while ... another team of robots tends to the passengers. Hmm, that's new. Maybe this is why Eternity Cruises can afford another ship. Why waste money on someone who needs to feed a family when you can build a bunch of machines that work all day without complaint? I'll be curious to see how well the bartender-bot functions. I paid a lot for that drink pass and I fully intend to reach a first-name basis. That metal bastard better be excited to see me after a few days.

I step off the gangway and into the ship, following Abigale as she completes her onboarding. She shuffles to the side and I find myself face-to-face with a greeter robot. Its humanoid shape is encased in a smooth white shell that separates at the joints, showing its black underframe. A pair of glowing blue eyes and a wide smile welcome my arrival.

"Greetings, passenger," it says in a human-like voice. "Name and room number, please."

"Nathan Lumon. D-23."

The robot pauses, then pings with error. "I'm sorry, D-23 is already occupied. Nor is there a Nathan Lumon registered as a passenger."

I consult my comdev ticket, swipe down to the room number, and give it a dramatic point. "D-23, says right here. Someone else is in my room."

"I'm sorry," the robot says. "D-23 is already occupied. Nor is there a Nathan Lumon registered—"

"Is there another room available?" Abigale says, inserting herself into the conversation.

"No. The ship is at full occupancy."

"Then add an occupant to mine," she says. "I have the extra space. Charge my account."

I start to respond, but Abigale shushes me.

"Charge complete," the robot says. "Welcome aboard, Nathan Lumon. Place your bags on the conveyor. They will be delivered to room A-2."

"A-2?" I say with surprise. A goddamn penthouse? I glance at Abigale, who gives me a sly wink. "Okay then." I toss my bags onto the conveyor belt nearby. Another robot snatches them and whisks away to my new penthouse. Wow. I have no idea what just happened, but I'm pretty sure I'll be satisfying a randy old lady by the end of the day.

Abigale hooks my arm like a door prize and escorts me through the entrance corridor. Ornate candelabras fill the space with a warm light. The red carpet beneath our feet is clean and vibrant, making us feel like celebrities. Hell, maybe Abigale *is* a celebrity. She did just comp a penthouse to a total stranger.

"Thank you," I say. "But why did you do that?"

She shrugs. "I have the money. Who am I to deny someone their grand departure?"

I squeeze her arm and chuckle. "So what are you, an heiress or something?"

"Yes, actually. My family owned a salvage company."

"Owned?"

"I'm the last surviving member. Cashed out, enjoyed my life, now I'm here."

"Good for you. I hope to live it up like that when I'm your age."

She laughs. "Well aren't you a funny one."

We stroll and banter until the passage opens up into a massive ballroom. The space is three stories tall, equally wide, and packed with opulence. My jaw slacks open as I drink in the scene. People of all shapes and sizes wander through the space, their every need tended to by a small army of robot servants. The entire perimeter is a cornucopia of fancy bars and posh restaurants. There's a notable lack of shops, but I assume they're tucked away to give the room a communal vibe. Gaudy chandeliers float overhead in a random dance. Their countless crystals toss beams of light around the room like ritzy disco balls.

Abigale guides me towards an escalator, not that I even notice. My widened eyes scan the extravagance like a young virgin at a whorehouse. The ballroom elevates as I do, and before I know it, we are tromping down the promenade deck. She seems to know exactly where to go (and what she wants, for that matter). It's kind of nice, to be honest. I have a penthouse *and* a personal guide.

As we round a corner, the entrance to the Sundial Lounge presents itself. A golden podium sits in front of two golden doors, all of which are framed by dark wood. It's fairly ostentatious, but I'll allow it. It's the kind of place I would normally dismiss, lest I suffer a blow to my plebeian ego. Abigale, on the other hand, is instantly greeted by the host. It's a robot, wearing a tuxedo, with a top hat and a fake mustache. Perfect day complete.

"Ms. Bennet," the robot says. "It's a pleasure to see you." It bows, then sways its hands towards the golden doors. "This way, please."

She smiles and nods her thanks.

"Should I be wearing a suit?" I ask with a sheepish tone.

Abigale pinches her homely duds. "Nobody cares on this ship."

"Okay then."

The robot escorts us through the foyer and into a lounge that is, to put it bluntly, obnoxiously classy. I have no right to be there. I'm a turd in a crystalline punchbowl. But wow, what a sight. Tufted leather booths, sculpted marble tables, intricate wood paneling, every inch a canvas to the gods. The backlit bar features bottles of nectar that cost more than I make in a year. I half expect to see a cigar-chomping casino mogul with mutton chops and—oh, there he is. I wave hello and he tips his hat.

Abigale guides me to a rounded booth and we take a seat. We scooch around the table and settle beside each other, close enough for her to squeeze my leg. Not gonna lie, I don't hate it. She has a brash gravitas that I can't find in women my own age. Maybe I'm not looking hard enough. Or maybe I shouldn't be gallivanting in thirsty nightclubs. In any case, it's just nice to have someone chase me for a change.

A robot waiter drops a pair of whiskeys onto the table.

We grab our glasses, clink them together, and take a sip.

"Fuck me," I say.

"Don't like it?" Abigale says.

I stare into my glass, stunned. "Precisely the opposite. This is the best goddamn drink that has ever touched my lips."

She smiles. "Hell of a way to start the trip, don't you think?"

I meet her gaze. "I am so glad I met you."

Her smile twists into a smirk and she offers another toast. We clink our glasses, enjoy another sip, and her hand slides up my thigh.

*   *   *

The penthouse is nice. Like, *really* nice. I know that's a stupid thing to say because a penthouse being nice is the entire damn point. But here's the thing. I have seen my share of luxury accommodations. I am a card-carrying member of the "keep the party going" crowd, which usually ends up in the richest person's suite.

But *this* is a level I had yet to experience.

I lean back against the plush headboard and scan the lavish interior. It has floor-to-ceiling port windows with sweeping views of the galaxy, a giant viewscreen as big as the bed, several leather sofas with sculpture-like tables, one-of-a-kind paintings, and the ultimate showpiece, a fully stocked bar with a dedicated robot bartender.

I named him Merl.

"Yo Merl," I say with gusto. "Another mimosa, please."

"Right away, sir," he says.

I sigh with satisfaction, then lift the sheet to inspect Little Nate. He's been very busy. Just finished plowing a woman twice his age for the fourth time. A shower is definitely in my near future. I also see that the bed stains are expanding with each session. Gross. As luck would have it, Merl is also our housekeeper. And chef. And concierge. Anything we want, Merl gets. What a way to spend a vacation.

Oh, and the sex is *great*.

I think Abigale is on a mission to see how many orgasms she can conjure in a single day. It's an admirable goal, one that I am more than happy to assist with. I thought for sure that she would be more docile and delicate, but I couldn't have been more wrong. She's a ravenous beast under the sheets. Serves me right. When it comes to the raw pleasures of living, it does seem that age is just a number.

Merl saunters over and drops a fresh mimosa on the side table.

"Thank you, Merl."

"You are most welcome, sir," he says with a butler-like tone.

"Anything else?"

"Yes, could you change the sheets after we get up?"

"Certainly, sir. Would you like an aromatic?"

"A what?"

"A pleasant smell infused into the new sheets."

I stare at him in contemplation, having never pondered such a thing. "Um, surprise me."

"Very good, sir." Merl bows and moseys back to the bar.

I pluck the champagne flute from the marble top and enjoy a lengthy sip. The resulting "aaaaah" rouses Abigale from a nap. She stirs under a thick duvet, then groans through a mild hangover. I technically have the same hangover, but my liver has taken far more abuse than hers. It barely registers, to be honest.

I should stop drinking, I think for the billionth time.

"Wakey wakey," I say.

"Eggs and bakey," she says from under the covers.

I chuckle, then get a sudden craving for breakfast.

"Merl," I say.

"Right away, sir," he says without needing further input.

Abigale pokes her head out and slithers her shoulders up the headboard. Her frizzy hair has gone full Einstein, which is both jarring and hilarious. She takes a needed breath, then grabs a fresh glass of water from her side table. I didn't even see Merl deliver it. What a guy. She downs the entire glass and clunks it back on the table. Great sex is tiring work. Gotta hydrate. She turns to me and smiles.

"How many peaks is that for you?" I say.

"Lost count," she says. "But I'm ready for more when you are."

"Jeez, Abby. You have a respectable appetite."

She shrugs. "Gotta get 'em while we still can."

A *month* of this? Wow. I don't think I have enough man juice.

"That reminds me," she continues. "What brings you to the grand departure?"

I glance at the nearest window, then return to Abigale. "We already departed."

"No, the *big* departure. You know, the supernova."

I scrunch my brow, clearly confused by the question.

Abigale gestures to Merl for another glass of water. He nods while plating a continental breakfast. "I have brain cancer," she says. "Stage four, inoperable. I went through the usual treatments, which gave me a brief remission. But it came back with a vengeance. I didn't feel like doing it again, so here I am. I'd rather go out with a bang, literally, than waste another day in the hospital." She turns to me. "What about you?"

I can only stare at her with my mouth agape.

"What's wrong?" she says.

"You're *dying?*"

"We're all dying."

"*I'm* not dying."

"But you're here."

"What the fuck difference does that make?"

"You're on the Starship Eternity."

I spread my arms, conveying a complete lack of sense.

She glances at Merl as if he's privy to a prank. After a brief ponder, she returns a puzzled gaze to me. "Where do you think we are right now?"

"On a month-long cruise to the Pinaman Cluster."

She cocks an eyebrow. "Let me see your ticket."

I grab my comdev from the table, bring up the record, and show it to her.

She studies the details for a moment, then huffs and shakes her head. "You're on the wrong ship, dingus."

"What do you mean? This is Eternity."

"This is *Starship* Eternity, not Eternity Cruises." She points at the logo.

My gaze detaches as the realization empties my lungs. I remember the port. The other Eternity ship. They didn't expand. That was *my* ship. I got into the wrong goddamn line. But it's not my fault. The guards told me to. Simple mistake. Easy fix.

"Merl," I say with a sudden urgency.

"Yes, sir," he says.

"Call the cockpit and tell them that I got on the wrong ship. We need to turn around."

"No can do, sir. The itinerary is automated and cannot be re-routed."

"But there's been a mistake."

"I'm sorry, sir."

"Don't be sorry, help me fix it."

"No can do, sir. The itinerary is automated—"

"And cannot be rerouted. Okay, fine. There are shuttles and such, yes?"

"No."

"What? Why not?"

"Because everyone on this ship is going to die," Abigale says.

A cold silence infects the room.

My chest swells as a violent dread consumes my mind. Abigale, sensing the fright, grabs my arm and grounds me to the space. Panic boils inside my stomach. But it's a reactive panic. An ignorant panic. There is a solution to be found. Calm the fuck down. I close my eyes, fight to regain composure, then refocus on Abigale.

"What is this place?" I say.

She frowns. "It's a suicide ship. Everybody on board is dying. As in, carrying a terminal diagnosis. Starship Eternity offers people like us a final hurrah. The ship is on its way to Baeron XF79, a red super-giant that is about to go supernova. We're going to park eight hours away from the blast wave, watch the show, and perish."

I glance at Merl. "Which is why the entire crew is robots."

"Correct."

"And why there are no shuttles or escape pods."

"Yup. Luxury is cheap. Safety is expensive."

The statement shocks me into silence.

"It's a pretty slick business model if you ask me," she says. "Trick out a basic starship with all the posh trappings, save money on all the regulatory bloat, then offer an exhilarating farewell to terminal patients with money to burn. It's a hedonistic voyage to the great beyond."

Merl saunters over with a large breakfast tray. He lowers it to the bed, unfolds a pair of frilly napkins, and bids us happy eating. It's an impressive spread, too. Three kinds of eggs, a selection of cured meats, steaming bread with numerous jams and butter, veggie juices, and a small tower of exotic fruits.

"Thank you," Abigale says, then dives in like a hungry badger.

Merl bows, then floats around the bed to drop a shot of whiskey onto my side table. That's some impressive room-reading. Merl stares at me in wait, as if intrigued by the situation. I grab the shot, toss it back, then hand the glass back to Merl. He plucks it from my grip, then reveals another shot like a street magician. Another toss, another pluck, and he saunters back to the bar. Dude gets me. Anyway, back to the whole death thing.

I ignore the tray of goodies. Scratch that. I grab a piece of bacon, then ignore the tray of goodies before rising out of bed. No pants or robe, just me and my swinging cock in the middle of an existential crisis. I shuffle to a port window and gaze out into the black abyss. How in the ever living fuck did I get here?

The mounting whiskey haze gives me a clue.

I was hungover as fuck and looked like death, which is why the entry guards pointed me to the wrong gangway. I was hungover as fuck and looked like death, which is why the boarding crew ignored the room discrepancy. I was hungover as fuck and looked like death, which is why Abigale procured some young dick for a final fling. I was hungover as fuck and looked like death, which is why I'm going to die in a supernova blast.

"I should stop drinking," I say.

And for the first time, I really mean it.

Regret hits me like a sledgehammer. I drop to the floor and begin to sob. What an image this is. A naked man crumpled on the ground, confronting the most damning life decision he has ever made. Couldn't wait one damn day for the next drink.

A soft hand grips my shoulder.

Abigale settles beside me, having risen from the sex cave and donned a robe. Merl had already stripped the bed before she walked over. She cradles me while crunching through a piece of bacon. Respect. I wail inside the embarrassing reality, a prison of my own making.

"Maybe there's something that can be done," she says gently.

"No can do, madam," Merl says from afar. "The itinerary is auto—"

"Shut the fuck up, Merl," Abigale says, whipping her head with a forceful tone.

"Yes, madam."

I whimper to a stop and wipe the snot from my face. I can feel the panic change. It withers and reforms. It's not hope. It's just ... a landing. I turn to Abigale. "How long do we have?"

"Two days."

My eyes return to the great black sea. Two days. I have two days to escape or die, the latter being most likely. Is it possible to speed-run through the stages of grief? Guess I'm about to find out. I exhale a measured breath and grasp Abby's hand. "Then let's make 'em count."

* * *

We have sex again. Because of course we do.

You cannot stare into the howling void without wanting to feel the exact opposite of terror. But now the terror is back, and with it comes an intense motivation for survival. If there is a way off this death ship, I'm going to find it. We're going to find it. And Merl is going to help us.

"Right, Merl?" I say.

"Come again, sir?" he says.

"Nothing, sorry. Thinking out loud."

"Very good, sir."

Abigale and I retreat to the giant lavatory and share a much-needed shower. The basin alone is bigger than my entire bathroom at home. I could host a poker game inside with enough space for a snack table. Multiple faucets overhead create a gentle rain of hot water. A blanket of steam swirls inside and whisks away before it becomes choking. The climate regulator is a new level of comfort. It's soothing, relaxing, and pleasantly distracting.

We have sex again. Because why not?

If it's truly the end, then there's wisdom in sharing a bounty of final pleasures. We actually talk through some good options while thrusting in the hot rain. At one point, a moaning climax morphs into a thought about disabling the autopilot. It's kinda sweet. And funny. And horrifying. Sweetly horrifying with a humorous twist.

Anyway.

We finish our sexy conclave and dry ourselves with pillow-soft towels. Powerful yet silent vents suck the steam from the bathroom, leaving clean mirrors and a crisp airflow. After some basic grooming, we clothe ourselves and return to the main living area where Merl rests in wait behind the bar. He lifts a bottle of top-shelf whiskey and tilts his head, signaling his willingness to serve. I wave it off and claim a stool at the bar.

Holy shit.

I declined.

Better late than never, I guess.

Abigale claims the stool beside me and the powwow begins.

"Okay then," I say, adding a judicious clap. "Let's hammer the facts. There are no shuttles or escape pods, right?"

"That is correct, sir," Merl says.

"Can we *make* an escape pod? Do you know of any airtight chambers on the ship that could double as a life raft?"

"No, sir. Even if you could repurpose a large container like a water tank or a freezer, your air supply would be severely limited. A few hours at most."

"What about distress beacons?" Abigale says.

"No, madam."

"Why not? They seem pretty standard. And cheap."

"The lack of distress beacons is a strategic decision. Should a passenger feel regret in their position, they cannot ruin the experience for the other passengers. The contract clearly states that once the ship departs, termination is guaranteed."

I sigh. "I assume that means no coms either."

"That is correct, sir."

"No escape, no rescue, what else do we have?"

"Can we disable the ship?" Abigale says with an uptick. "Kill the engines and hope that a salvage crew finds us? Or hell, even change course?"

"Impossible, madam. Also a strategic decision. There are no cockpit controls. The engine room is detached from the main compartments. It is magnetically sealed and would require a spacewalk to access."

"Lemme guess," I say. "No spacesuits."

"That is correct, sir."

"What about the crew?" Abigale says. "Robots don't need spacesuits."

"Irrelevant, madam. We do not have the tools or protocols to initiate a shutdown or course correction. Again—"

"A strategic decision."

"Correct, madam."

"Well fuck me sideways," I say and slump across the bar.

An awkward silence settles between us.

"Might I suggest," Merl says, "a walk around the promenade to take in the sights? The central ballroom has several options for fine dining."

I lift my head from the counter and give Merl a stink eye. "You're a real buzzkill, you know that?"

"Thank you, sir."

"That's not a compliment."

"Then I apologize, sir."

"He's not wrong, though," Abigale says.

My head tilts towards her, cautiously intrigued.

"Two days is a long time. Let's go get a steak. We can plan or wallow later."

I crack a genuine smile. It's a strange feeling, to be honest. Here I am, ticking down to the ultimate doom and powerless to intervene.

At least for now. But at the moment, this strange and surreal moment, I think I'm ... happy. A steak really does sound good. With fries. And asparagus. And Abby across the table. And a tall glass of sparkling water.

* * *

I cut through a slab of medium-rare meat with the ease of slicing butter. The flesh on my fork is flakey, tender, and smells like a dream. I stare at it for a time. How long, I cannot say. It's just so perfect. The experience feels heightened. Amplified. I'm a small boy again, unwrapping my first piece of candy. I bring the fork to my lips and press the meat to my tongue. A truly unique flavor invades my tastebuds and fireworks explode in my brain. My eyes close and I enjoy the show. So vibrant. So delectable. It is, by a very wide margin, the single most delicious thing I have ever tasted.

"Better save some of that moaning for me," Abby says.

My eyes open and I chuckle with embarrassment. "Sorry. I've never had brevokia before, let alone from Gruvenna. It's like nothing I've ever tasted."

"You should never be sorry for enjoying a good experience."

"Cheers to that."

We lift our flutes of sparkling water, clink them together, and take a sip.

"Are you sure you don't want something stiffer?" I say.

"No," she says. "I'm actually enjoying the clarity. The meal tastes better, the vibe feels richer, and make no mistake, I am going to *wreck* the dessert cart."

We share a laugh.

My gaze floats around the establishment, a posh steakhouse nestled inside the central ballroom. The tables are packed with smiling faces and joyous demeanors. The looming doom feels distant, almost artificial. It hits me that every soul I see is destined to die in the near future. Disease will take them. They cannot run, they cannot hide, they cannot bribe death for another day. One might assume that the ship would devolve into debauchery, but the passengers remain tethered to decorum. All they want is togetherness, contentment, a blissful detachment from the trappings of normal life. I have never seen anything so beautiful.

"So if you *were* dying of something," Abby says, "what do you think it would be?"

"Huh," I say as a placeholder. I guess I hadn't thought about death very much up to this point, aside from the usual *hope I don't get hit by a bus* mental default. I never consider risk. I never consider health or genetics. I don't think about exercise or nutrition. Maybe I should. Hell, maybe I *am* dying. "If I had to guess, I'd say colon cancer."

"Family history?"

"Yup. Three of my grandparents died of it. My father already had it, but caught it soon enough to have it surgically removed."

"I assume you get regular colonoscopies then."

"Nope."

Abby stops chewing and glares at me.

"I know," I say with a hint of guilt. "Given my history, I should have started getting them ten years ago. Seemed like too much of a hassle. And here's the kicker, I haven't seen a doctor since I was a teenager. I dunno. I guess it never struck me as important."

"The invincibility of youth."

"Yeah, but I'm not a youth anymore."

"Yet you still live like one."

I shrug. "Don't know any other way."

"That's a handy excuse."

I start to retort, but sigh and nod instead. She's right. And that lifestyle is why I'm stuck on a doom ship. "It's a hell of a lesson, that's for sure."

"Better late than never."

"Cheers to that."

We clink our glasses again and enjoy another sip.

"Does this mean I'm an adult now?" I say.

Abby snort-laughs some water through her nose.

* * *

Day One ends with a futile argument between myself and a robot manager. A manager of what, I have no idea, but that's what its ID plate says. I ask the same questions and get the same answers. No leads, no ideas, no realistic options of any kind. I feel like a detective trapped in a prison cell. What good is deduction if there is nothing to deduce? And yet, I have another full day ahead of me. I'm not one to quit, but this is feeling more and more like an unscalable wall. Death is skipping along beside me, giddy as a schoolgirl with a crush.

Once again, I lay in bed with Abby.

She's already asleep and I'm staring at the ceiling. I have no plan, so there's not much to think about other than my own demise. It must be so comforting, knowing that your pain and suffering will go away soon. It'll just vanish with the dullness of a light switch. From afar, a giant wall of fire will consume a miniscule dot, and the grand experiment will come to an end. Dark, silent, complete. I guess I have my own pain and suffering, just not with a diagnosis. Is that my only separation? Maybe I am on the right ship.

That'll do until tomorrow.

It's another day, after all.

* * *

My eyelids slowly rise, bringing my final slumber to an end. Waking up for the last time, and knowing it's the last time, is a hell of a thing. The last time I will ever smack my lips and swallow, relieving a dry throat. The last time I will ever groan into a stretch, relieving muscle aches. The last time I will ever rise like a zombie and press my feet to the floor. This must be what it feels like for a death row inmate on the day of execution.

But I was wrongfully convicted.

And no one gives a shit.

Aside from Abby.

I glance over my shoulder to the pile of covers on the other side of the bed. Abby will also rouse to her final day, but she made peace with it long ago. She may as well be rising to another day of retirement. She will toil in the garden, enjoy a tasty lunch, watch a movie, and shuffle off her mortal coil without fear or trepidation. I'm happy for her. I'm also jealous. I have said in the past that I do not fear death, only pain. Given that framework, I shouldn't be afraid. But I am. I guess a better framework would be that I do not fear a sudden death. But an unexpected death that I can see on approach? That is truly horrifying.

The intercom pings with an incoming announcement.

"Attention all passengers," says a voice from overhead. "If you would direct your attention to the starboard side of the ship, we have arrived at the Baeron XF79 star system. The core collapse of the red supergiant is imminent, calculated within the next two hours. Observation platforms are available at the bow and stern, both of which will be serving drinks and refreshments. All port windows have been filter-treated, so you can safely observe the coronal ejection. The eight-hour countdown will begin upon collapse. Please enjoy the show and the subsequent obliteration. Once again, we thank you for choosing Starship Eternity."

The intercom pings with completion and I am left staring at the windows. The glowing dot in the distance stares back at me. It doesn't hate, it doesn't judge, it just is. We came to it for help. And help it will. I do regret never delving into philosophy. In this moment, this ugly and absurd moment, I yearn for the perspectives of great thinkers.

I glance behind me again and find Abby awake, staring at the ceiling with a smile on her face. It's strangely cute, like a kid about to depart for summer camp.

"How are you feeling?" I say.

"Content," she says.

"Not happy?"

"Happiness is too abstract. I'm happy when I eat a good meal. I'm happy when I get to see a close friend." She tosses me a sly grin. "I'm happy when we have sex."

I blush in response.

"But they're all different in the moment," she says. "Happiness isn't tangible. It's a blind chase down a dark road. Contentment, on the other hand, is *real*. It's a solid state of mind. It's like landing on a pillow instead of floating through the clouds."

"Huh," I say with an uptick. "So you're my philosopher."

"Come again?"

"Nothing. Just dumping a regret."

She smirks. "I think you misheard me."

I think for a moment, then chuckle. "Oh."

* * *

I'm just going to say it. In the last two days, I have had the best sex of my life. Hands down, bar none, nowhere near a close second. There is something so delightfully liberating about being with someone who knows who they are, what they want, and isn't afraid to ask for it.

Alas, it is within this revelation that I have identified another life regret. Age should have never entered my sexual equation. What good is smooth skin if the sex sucks? I shudder to think of how many glorious rendezvous I denied myself. But at the same time, I am grateful for having discovered true pleasure before the end.

Once again, we are sweaty, exhausted, and staring at the ceiling.

Merl, ever vigilant, has already started prepping a tasty lunch.

"So," I say, "where would you like to watch the show? Bow or stern?"

"Neither," she says, then gestures to the wall of windows.

"I figured you would want to get dressed up and dance to the end."

"I'm done with all that. I've had my fill of other people, to be honest. In fact, this is why I booked this particular suite. Starboard side, full view of the show, just me and my final thoughts all the way to the finale."

I pause for thought, then come to the exact same conclusion.

Why would I waste my final moments dealing with other people's emotions? There's going to be cheering, weeping, panic, and everything in between. The last thing I want is for my grand exit to be polluted by someone else's hang-ups. Fuck them. I'm where I want to be.

"That said," she continues, "I didn't expect to have a companion."

The statement twists my stomach. "Oh shit, I am so sorry. I had no intention of spoiling this for you. I can leave if you want."

"No, no, no," she says and grips my arm. "You misunderstand. I didn't expect it, but I am thrilled to have it." Her tone softens and her hand slips down to mine. "My husband died ten years ago. I loved him deeply, and I still miss him. The loneliness of the last decade has been crushing. I feel it on my chest every day. I'm not afraid of being alone, or loving again. I just miss his laugh. I miss his voice. I miss his terrible jokes." Her watering eyes detach from mine and float to the windows. "I miss him, Nate. And I am so grateful that I can tell you that."

The room falls into a solemn silence.

"Hey," I say softly. "Do you know how many ears Captain Kirk has?"

She turns to me, confused.

"Three. The left ear, the right ear, and the final frontier."

Abby snorts into laughter, which gets me laughing as well. Tears drip from her cheeks and onto the sheets. I can only hope they're steeped in serenity.

Moments later, the room fills with a blinding light.

It stifles the laughter and hooks our undivided attention to the windows. We stare into the wall of white with a full understanding of what it means. The core has collapsed. And right on cue, a hologram timer appears and begins its eight-hour countdown. The window filter darkens and the brightness dissipates, leaving a glowing ball of fire in the distance. Abby squeezes my hand as we watch in humbled silence.

* * *

Here's something I never thought I would say. Supernovas are boring. I am gazing into the universe's most glorious fireworks show, and all I can think about is my own disappointment. I even donned a robe and walked up to the window to get a closer look. That's right, I closed the gap between myself and an exploding star by 20 feet, thinking it would help. But all I see is a little circle expanding at a leisurely pace. I know it's going to get bigger. Before long, it will be the only thing we can see. But for now, I just can't swallow the letdown. I glance at the timer and sigh that only two hours have passed.

"This is dumb," I say to my impending death.

"I know, right?" Abby says from the bed. She plucks another fry from her plate. "I didn't expect to lose interest so soon."

"It's kinda like waiting for a band to play their one big hit."

"On the bright side, the burger is delicious."

"Thank you, madam," Merl says from the bar.

"Hey, Merl," I say. "Can you bring the shuttle around? I'm bored and want to go home."

"No can do, sir. The itinerary is automated and—"

"Just messing with you, dude."

"Ah, and a cracking joke it was. Bravo."

"You know what's weird?" I say while turning to Abby. "Had I known this was coming, I thought for sure that I would spend the last hours of my life in a hedonistic spiral. I would drink, snort, and puff my way into oblivion. I would dance on the bar, sing like a banshee, fuck anyone willing, and greet the end of all things in a kaleidoscopic stupor. And if I were lucky, I would pass out happy and never wake up."

"You can still do that," Abby says and points at the door.

"Yeah," I say, then wander back to the bed. I drop the robe, get under the covers, and lean back against the headboard. "So why is that suddenly unappealing?"

Abby shrugs. "People change. Values change. What's important today will be irrelevant tomorrow."

"But there is no tomorrow."

"True. So what *do* you want to do?"

I think for a moment, then turn to the bar. "Hey, Merl."

"Yes, sir?"

"Do you have a chessboard?"

"I do, sir. In fact, there are several tabletop games to choose from. I am well-versed in all and can serve as an instructional guide for your adventure. Shall I construct a list of popular titles and fetch the rulebooks?"

"No. Chess is great. And a selection of snacks."

"Right away, sir."

I turn to Abby and grip her hand. "I want to sit here with you, play chess in bed, eat bonbons, and talk about whatever enters our minds. That sounds like a perfect ending."

She smiles. "That does sound perfect."

We lean in for a kiss.

"One problem, though," she says.

"You don't know how to play?"

"Oh no, quite the opposite. I'm going to destroy you. I just don't want you to be all sad and whiny when you die without a win."

I lean back and chuff. "Game. Fucking. On."

*　*　*

Abby wasn't lying. She's an exceptional chess player. I lost the first game so quickly that it made my balls shrink. I learned that she was highly ranked during her youth and used the game as a means to deal with family issues. Her parents were brilliant business types who demanded excellence. She wanted to sharpen her mind through chess, and ended up sharpening the daggers that she plunged into every opponent. I received one of those daggers during the second game.

And the third game.

And the fourth game.

Sigh.

But I'm getting better. We have both played our entire lives and have the capacity to learn each other's methods. Her game is much deeper than mine, but at least I stand a chance. That elusive win has become my all-consuming life goal. Granted, I only have a few hours to achieve it, but it feels like a perfect use of time.

"Checkmate," Abby says.

"Dammit," I say, then knock over my king.

"You shouldn't have moved your bishop."

I stare at the board and mentally play out the mistake. "Shit."

"That was close, though. I think you're zeroing in on my mid-game."

"Merl, prep the shuttle. I need to go home and practice."

"No can do, sir. The itinerary is—"

"Joking, dude. Jeez."

"Ah, a perfectly executed yuk. Well done, sir."

Abby giggles and starts resetting the board for the next game.

I glance at the wall of windows, where a giant disc of fire has slowly overtaken most of the visual field. The poles have vanished behind the floor and ceiling. I can clearly see the churning storm, a cauldron of flame that will incinerate every inch of the ship. With the full understanding that my body will be reduced to atoms in the very near future, I cannot help but feel a cleansing coming over me. Every action I have taken will be forgotten. Every regret I have carried will be erased. None of them matter. None of them ever mattered. And even if I had led a life of great consequence, one with a legacy that endured for eons, only now do I realize that none of it will survive the heat death of the universe.

"Your move," Abby says.

I snap back to the moment and open with my knight.

"Wow," she says. "Look at you pulling out a Reti."

"I got a plan."

She smiles. "Let's hope it works."

And so we play again.

I make a move, and we chat about our favorite movies. She makes a move, and we reveal the most defining moments of our lives. I make a move, and we talk about my father's struggle with addiction. She makes a move, and we discuss the enduring sorrow of outliving her daughter. I make a move, and we gossip about Merl's snack selection. She makes a move, and we delve into the great unknowns of the universe. On and on we go, recreating the stories of our lives with every pluck and move. Our tapestry grows as the chessboard wanes. Towards the end of our exchange, only a handful of pieces remain.

The ship begins to rumble.

We glance at the windows, now fully engulfed by fire.

Our eyes meet again as a shared peace washes over us.

Without looking, I move my queen a few spaces forward. "Checkmate."

Abby smiles. "Good game."

We embrace, close our eyes, and bask inside a warm cocoon, content and complete.

THE END

Every truth demands a sacrifice.

The first humans have landed on Mars, and while the world is united in awe, Dan is busy flirting at a casino pub. A beautiful woman captures his attention. She is receptive to his charm, but to close the deal, he must submit to a painful audit.

THE SURVEY

The Golden Calf was an average casino that attracted average people. It occupied a lonely block away from the main strip and often served as a waypoint for wealthy tourists. Glamour passed through, but never stayed. It filled a particular niche, one where the drinks were cheap, the smoke was thick, and the music dulled the pain. The games still offered a lure of possibility, but inside the Calf, they were steeped in self-loathing.

Several bars and restaurants were scattered throughout, but one hallowed pub was a haven for the crushed and battered. The Mule was a beacon of sorts, shining its hazy light on the ruins of excess. It was never empty, as the main strip was a ravenous demon that extracted its daily bounty. The resulting conclave was an ever-churning mass of broken people recanting broken dreams. Every person had a story, and every story had an ear.

Thus, when a diamond entered the rough, it drew attention.

A beautiful woman in a white evening gown strolled into the room. Conversations quieted as the ethereal figure floated through the space. Her blonde hair was teased into an elegant style, a deliberate effort that took time and focus. A small silver purse dangled from her gloved hands. She let it sway loosely, showing little fear of the surroundings. Her sapphire eyes scanned the interior with mild inter-est. They met several stares, but did not react. The woman was there on purpose, much to the cautious intrigue of everyone present.

Before long, she arrived at an empty table. It was a random two-seater along the rear wall with a pair of tufted loungers. She pulled a finger across the table surface, staining the tip of her glove with un-told days of filth. Lifting it for study, she rubbed the dirt with her thumb before swiftly losing interest. She removed the gloves, tucked them into the purse, and took a seat. Facing outward, she crossed one leg over the other and scanned the dank interior, paying no mind to the sea of curious eyes.

Her gaze floated through the smoke and over to the central bar. A pair of androids in black tuxedos tended to a throng of thirsty pa-trons. The robots were sturdy types with exoskeletons, not the slick pseudo-humans who wandered the strip. It made sense given the location. Drunken fools can do serious damage to expensive droids, especially ones with lab-grown skin. Best to save money and bartend with robot bouncers.

Thankfully, there wasn't much fight in the crowd that night. Sev-eral had given their attention to a row of televisions above the bar, all of which displayed the same feed. It was a momentous day, after all. The first human beings had set foot on Mars. The main event had occurred earlier that morning and every news station was streaming it on a loop. The astronauts arrived safely, a foot touched soil, some words were said, and now the world was stuck with the same footage until the crew constructed a base. Most of the world had already lost interest. Even the biggest moments failed to hold the modern atten-tion span.

The woman watched the watchers with a sense of pity. She won-dered if they felt anything at all. Moments later, a man approached the table.

He was handsome by pub standards, but decidedly average out in the wild. His suit was ill-fitted, likely purchased off the rack. Same for the shoes, watch, and tie. He wore a deliberately messy hairstyle, no doubt to attract the edgy women who wandered in by accident. This was his lair, and a rare lioness had entered.

The man sauntered up to the table with a trite swagger. He donned a frisky smile as his eyes combed the woman from head to toe. "Do you need help getting to the right meadow?"

She glanced up and met his gaze. "Come again?"

"You're clearly in the wrong spot."

"Am I?"

"Well," he said, "you only need one eye to see the filth in this swamp. Or hell, no eyes and a functioning nostril."

The woman cracked a smile.

"Aha," he said with an uptick. "A sense of humor, the only tonic in a place like this. Maybe you are in the right spot. May I join you with some drinks?"

The woman glanced around the pub again. All eyes had detached from her presence and returned to their previous chatter. Privacy had returned, at least for a moment. "Sure," she said, then motioned to the other chair.

The man turned to the bar and lifted two fingers, prompting a nod from the android tender. He removed his suit jacket, draped it across the chair back, and claimed the seat. The old leather popped and cracked as he settled into the cushion. He matched her crossed legs, then slowly leaned back and folded his hands. It was a practiced maneuver, one that conveyed a familiar comfort. Unseen to the tipsy fool, but loud and clear to a lioness.

"Dan," he said, and reached across the table.

"Julia," she said after a brief pause, then completed the shake.

"If I may be so bold," he said with a coy grin, "how did an angel like you end up in a hell like this?"

"So this is hell?"

"Not by my definition," he said as a quick retort. "I like to think of this place as more of a purgatory. If heaven is the strip, then hell is the airport."

The woman snickered.

"Ah, she can laugh too. That's nice."

The android arrived with a pair of Old Fashioneds in branded lowball glasses. It set them on the table and nodded at the man before taking its leave.

"Thank you, Pete," Dan said.

The android did not respond.

The woman eyed the amber liquid. The bourbon was decent, that much she could tell. Not great, but enough to avoid the creep-factor of bottom-shelf booze. A dark cherry with a twisted orange peel rested atop a single large ice cube. The man was careful to convey basic class. Be that as it may, she reached across the table and claimed the drink closest to him. She lifted the glass, gestured her thanks, and took a sip.

"No offense taken," he said.

"A girl can never be too careful."

"In a place like this, I understand." He winked, then lifted the other glass and took a sip.

"So why do you frequent The Mule?"

"Frequent? Nah, more like ... occasionally haunt."

Julia cocked an eyebrow, clearly unconvinced.

Dan rapped his fingers on the table before switching to a more somber tone. "The Mule is a *real* place. Inside these walls, people drop the mask. They don't come here to perform. They come here to recover. And I come here for them. It's the only place I can get a real conversation."

Julia thought for a moment, then smiled and raised her glass. "Cheers to realness."

Dan mirrored the smile. "I'll drink to that," he said, then clinked his glass to hers.

They shared another sip and the tension suddenly abated.

"So in all seriousness," Dan said, "you look like a pearl in a sea of oysters. There must be a good story that got you through these doors."

"I hate to disappoint, but I'm simply here on business."

"Business?" Dan said with a chuckle. "What possible business has you dressing like that?" Answering his own question, he leaned in for a more subtle exchange. "I doubt that anyone in here can afford your wares."

"That's a hell of an assumption to make," she said with mild offense.

"Then dispel it for me."

She stared at him for several seconds, allowing his mind to wander. His eyes were genuinely curious, not just yearning for sexual banter. Dan was out of his element, but he wasn't a predator. Just a normal guy trying to get laid. He had enough wherewithal to preen his feathers and prance about. It was oddly charming, like a chicken pretending to be a peacock.

He was perfect.

"I'm conducting a survey," Julia said.

"A survey? For whom?"

"My employer prefers to remain anonymous."

Dan raked his gaze across the hideous pub. "No surprise there."

"I have instructions to seek a particular type of person and ask them ten questions. At which point, I have been authorized to award them a substantial prize."

"Interesting," he said with a cheeky grin. "Can I help you find this person?"

"You already have."

Dan perked with attention. He sat up in the chair, straightened his tie, and pointed at himself, asking the question without asking the question.

Julia nodded.

"Well then," he said. "I am suddenly very happy that I hit on you."

"You weren't before?"

Dan stammered in response. "Let's just say that someone of your quality rarely graces this establishment. I was firmly prepared to kick rocks."

She smirked. "And now you're my plaything."

"In more ways than one, I hope." The cheeky grin returned.

Julia bit her lower lip and offered a slight grunt. "Tell you what, let's get through the survey and we'll see where the evening leads."

"Sounds delightful." Dan leaned back and took another sip. "So what do I have to do?"

"Just sit there. I'm going to ask you ten questions and you are going to answer me. All I ask is that you take them seriously and answer honestly."

"I can do that."

"Ready to begin?"

"Right now? You don't need a notepad or anything?"

She pressed a finger to her temple.

"You must have a fantastic memory."

"I do."

Dan was taken aback, but kept his cool. "Okay then, let's do this."

Julia adjusted her posture to a more inquisitive stance, like an old college professor on a coffee break. Her demeanor shifted. The flirtatious air evaporated, replaced by a cold gravity. Dan stiffened and held his breath. His foot was in the door, but now he wondered if it should have been.

"Question one," she said flatly. "What do you enjoy most in life?"

Dan laughed. "That's the kind of question you ask? Fuck me, I thought I was about to be psychoanalyzed or something."

Julia did not respond.

"Sorry, just releasing the pressure." Dan shifted a bit and cleared his throat. "If I had to say, nothing beats a stiff drink and the touch of a beautiful woman." He lifted his glass and winked, obviously pleased with his answer.

"Sex and alcohol?" she said with a half-grin. "That's your answer?"

"You said to be honest."

"I did. And you were. And I thank you. Moving on."

Dan finished his drink and motioned for another. The stigma was swift and palpable, but the only play was to own it. He liked what he liked, no shame in that.

"Question two," she said. "What do you enjoy most about living on this planet?"

Dan narrowed his gaze. "That's the same question."

"Is it?"

"Yes. How is it not?"

"Then would your answer be the same?"

Dan paused for a quick deliberation. "Yes."

"Sex and alcohol."

"Yes."

"Noted."

Dan squirmed in his chair.

"Question three. What are you most proud of?"

"How do you mean?"

Sensing the discomfort, Julia reached across the table and touched his hand. She smiled and softened her tone. "It's not a trick question. It's meant in any way you wish. Don't think about it too hard. There's no wrong answer." She rubbed his skin, then pulled away.

Dan exhaled with relief. *She's playing her part*, he thought. *Just be yourself.*

The android arrived with a fresh cocktail. Without breaking stride, it delivered the drink and snatched the empty glass. Dan plucked the beverage and took a heavy glug. The current question was proving troublesome. He mused while swirling the amber liquid, sorting through a barrage of cheesy answers. The pondering ended with a grunt and grin. "If I had to say, it would be my 1987 Porsche 911. It's out in the garage if you fancy a ride."

"Your mode of transportation?"

"That's an odd way to put it, but yes. It's the car I always wanted and it took me a long time to find it. I'm proud of it and I keep it in pristine condition. And again, a cruise down the strip is on the table, should you like one."

Julia did not respond. She stared at the man through a cold expression, infecting the space between them with a dreadful anticipation. "Question four. Where does your daughter rank on your list of prideful things?"

His grin quickly faded. "What?"

"Your daughter, Emma. Sixteen years old. Star student. Currently enrolled in numerous advanced placements and scouting for colleges. Where does she rank?"

Dan scoffed and shook his head. "Survey my ass. What are you, a private sleuth? Is that bitch looking for child support again?"

"Question five. Did you know that your wife cried herself to sleep for six straight months after the divorce?"

"I'm not playing this g—"

"And yet, you wanted to keep gambling. She stood by your side for three years before divorce became the only option. Counseling, therapy, intervention, nothing worked. You drained the bank accounts and left them both destitute. And so she cried for six months. But then she rose from the ruins and built a new life, for her and your daughter. You, on the other hand, fled into the arms of a prostitute named Chloe. You both spent the money, your wife's money, your daughter's future tuition, on drugs and designer clothing. You even paid for an abortion. Another girl."

Dan stared at Julia with a mixture of shock and anger. His lips tightened as his knuckles knocked on the table. Without a word, he snatched his drink and shot to his feet, shoving the chair into the wall. The resulting scrape and clunk hooked several eyes around them. He raised a finger and bared his teeth, but the damage was done. He huffed in disgust, then turned away and vanished into the smoky interior.

Julia had not flinched. The scene had garnered some looks and mumbles, but she ignored them. She did not stir to leave. The table remained a playground and her cocktail remained tasty. She simply relaxed and enjoyed some casual sips, undeterred by the exit.

Moments later, Dan returned.

He stopped at the table and loomed over the woman, wearing his threat for all to see. This was his bar, his show, his rules. How dare she undermine that sacred fact. His face was taut, but his arms were twitching nervously by his side. One hand clutched a new drink. The other twisted over itself like a sickly snake.

"How did you know?" he said.

"Which part?"

"The abortion. How did you know? We paid in cash, used fake names, no cameras or paperwork. We never told anyone. It doesn't exist."

"It's my job to know."

Dan took a measured breath, then clunked the drink on the table and returned to his seat. He maintained eye contact as his racing brain struggled to make sense of the situation.

"Everything is still in play," Julia said. "The reward, the fun, everything. All you need to do is complete the survey."

"And what if I refuse?"

"This is not mandatory. You can walk away at any time. The prize, on the other hand, will remain with me. I'm sure someone else will be happy to claim it."

Dan nodded slowly, but did not shed his apprehension. "Okay. Continue."

"So where were we?" she said with a slight uptick. "Ah yes, question six. Why do you knowingly inflict pain on others?"

He opened his mouth to respond, but halted abruptly. The bullshit, the spin, the retaliation, it all congealed inside his throat. None of it mattered. She knew. Honestly was the only way across the finish line. His gaze fell to the table, where his fist unraveled and slithered around the sweaty drink. He lifted it for another sip, then gently returned the glass to the surface. "Because if I have to suffer, then others should too."

"You feel they deserve it."

"Don't we all?"

"Interesting."

Dan did not retort, opting to let the answer lie.

"Question seven," she said after a brief pause. "When did you realize that you were capable of being cruel?"

An immediate chill crept around his body, but he did not react. His eyes closed as an early memory flooded his mind. He could smell the grass, taste the pollen, hear the other kids around the yard. It was a moment of pure indulgence, one that he never understood as right or wrong. "I stabbed my friend in the eye." His lungs emptied, as if to finally understand the implication. "I can still hear the screams, the frantic parents, the chaos. I remember the bloody ooze and how it leaked down his face. They blamed everything but me, of course. I was just a kid. There were seminars at school about the evils of video games, music, and all that stuff. I can clearly recall that sense of power. It was a life-changing calamity, all because of me. I loved that feeling, and I never forgot it."

"Power begets cruelty," Julia said with a solemn tone. "And the cruel seek power. They are two sides of the same coin."

Dan chewed on his tongue as a grim reality infected his mind. The beast within was a beast indeed, and he had fed it all his life. It was a realization worth exploring, a painful awareness that needed extermination. But now was not the time. After a long and grueling ponder, he swallowed the shame and motioned to continue.

"Question eight," she said. "On the grand spectrum of human quality, ten being the best, and one being the worst, where would you place yourself?"

Dan crossed his arms and straightened his back, as if to give the question a proper mulling. His head lifted from its slump and gazed around the pub. Countless scenes emerged from the past, many of which had claimed permanent dark holes in his memory. No joy, no laughter, only the howling void of sorrow. He turned to Julia and rested his elbows on the table. The question, it would seem, had struck a slumbering nerve.

"Three," he said.

"Interesting. Why not two or one?"

He drew a deep breath and released it slowly. "I know a guy. A preacher. He runs a church on the outskirts of town. His congregation is the poorest of the poor. Many of them don't have running water or electricity. And yet, he openly tells them that God wants him to drive a Rolls-Royce. He buys a new one every few years, using money given to him by people who can't afford to buy food. It's the same Rolls-Royce, mind you, that he drives into town to solicit underage prostitutes." Dan sighed and nodded. "I know a two."

Julia frowned slightly, but dared not interrupt.

"I also know a guy," Dan continued, "who raises pit bulls for an underground dog fighting ring. That's bad enough, but he also tortures them, brutally, to elevate their aggression. I've seen it with my own eyes, and it's, um ... harrowing. And because he's so successful, he's lauded in that world. This is a man who torments innocent creatures to elevate his own status." His face tightened with anger. "I know a one."

They stared at each other in a moment of shared disgust. Julia glanced away and shook her head, offering a brief commiseration. Regardless of where the survey would lead, or how they stood to benefit, they could at least acknowledge the horrors of true depravity.

"Question nine," she said with a softer voice. "Would you consider yourself a typical human, or an anomaly?"

Dan chuckled into a sigh. "Lady, I know more threes than I can count. We're everywhere. We lie, cheat, and steal to get what we want." He tossed his hands up and fell back in the chair. "In fact, I can't recall ever meeting a truly selfless person. I have met many who claim to be, but they're all so obviously hollow. They just learn to say the right things." Dan scrunched his brow, trying to find a mental port of harbor. "Maybe there is such a thing as a selfless hero. I would like to think there is, but if life has taught me anything, it's that goodness gets you nowhere. It's the assholes who thrive. The rest are treading water." His eyes widened and locked onto Julia, as if to enjoy a breakthrough in therapy.

"Good," she said.

Dan finished his drink, then lowered it to the table and nudged it away with a finger. His hands folded as he awaited an unknown fate.

"Are you ready for the final question?"

He shrugged. "As ready as I'll ever be."

"It's a doozy. The fate of your species depends on it."

"*My* species?" His eyes narrowed.

"Human beings are on the verge of unlocking interstellar travel. There are not one, but two companies building generational spaceships right now. Which means, the first humans that will leave the solar system are alive *today*."

Dan sat in quiet contemplation.

"You see," Julia continued, "when humans reach the next star system, they will have joined an elite fraternity of spacefaring civilizations. They will be contacted by an alliance of cultures, at which point, human culture will spread throughout the cosmos."

"I'm not hearing a question."

Julia leaned forward and crossed her arms on the table. Her eyes hardened, infecting the space with gravitas. "But here's the kicker. You have made it abundantly clear that the average human is a greedy, selfish, whorish, unreliable deadbeat. So the tenth and final question is this: does humanity deserve to colonize space?"

Dan stared into nothingness as a sense of dread invaded his conscience. His shoulders slumped. The noisy pub faded into the background. They were alone inside a bubble, a prison known only to them. Julia stared at him with a cold intensity, awaiting the answer. One word. One moment of truth and integrity.

"No," he said.

"Why not?"

"We haven't earned it. We trash our home, we trash ourselves, we trash the ones we love. We're so painfully lost." He turned to the crowd and pointed at various people. "That man is cheating on his wife. That woman is stealing from her company. That man lies to his best friend to fleece him for money. That woman cons the elderly." He sulked and sighed. "And I know this because I scammed them all for fake investments."

An awkward silence settled between them.

Dan bowed his head and shouldered the guilt.

Julia slapped the table and resumed a playful demeanor. "Very good," she said with a toothy smile.

The sudden shift in tone caught Dan by surprise. "Wait, what? That's it?"

"Yes. You have completed the survey and earned your reward. Are you ready for it?"

Dan, still bemused, offered a single nod.

Julia reached into her purse and retrieved a small box. The matte black exterior consumed the light, like a tiny black hole. She opened the lid to reveal two pills. After plucking one for herself, she slid the box across the table and offered the other to Dan.

"What is this?" he said.

"Playtime," she said, adding a flirtatious wink. She tossed the pill into her mouth and followed it with a sip.

A wave of relief flooded his body. It was a bloody good prank, one that left him feeling a bit sheepish. Even he, it would seem, was susceptible to a well-crafted grift. He still wondered how she knew so much about him, but then again, that's the nature of the digital beast. He, too, could learn as much as he needed with a few knowing clicks. That's how the game worked. Find the weak points and leverage them for payment. She was a master, and his newfound respect was morphing into desire. He plucked the pill and swallowed it dry. A delirious romp was just what he needed.

"Congratulations," Julia said.

"For what?" Dan said, returning the wink.

"You are now patient zero for the final plague."

His amorous glow faded to black.

"It works quickly," she continued. "In 30 minutes, you will experience fever and nausea. In 60 minutes, your nervous system will begin to fail. You will become mentally erratic and seek help out of panic. The pathogen is highly contagious, highly resilient, and spreads rapidly. In 90 minutes, you will bleed from every hole in your body. The pain will be immeasurable as blood seeps into your joints, rendering you immobile. In 120 minutes, all critical systems will fail. Your lungs will collapse and you will die gasping."

Dan glared at her with his mouth agape.

"In one week," she continued, "the world economy will collapse. In two weeks, half the population will be dead. In three weeks, civilization will collapse. In four weeks, the human experiment will be over and the species will have been eradicated." She lingered on the point, then raised a hand and chuckled. "Well, except for those poor bastards on Mars. But it's not like they can rush back and repopulate the planet."

Dan was frozen in horror, but then he pointed at Julia and laughed. "Ha! Good one. You have a way with terrifying words, that's for sure."

"You don't believe me?"

"Of course not. You popped a pill too."

"That's because I won't be alive for long enough to suffer the effects. I just needed you to trust me in the moment."

Dan stuttered, searching for any lick of sense.

"And with that," Julia said, "I bid you and your species a fond farewell." She reached into her purse and withdrew a small pistol. Pressing it to her temple, she offered one last smile and pulled the trigger. The blast tore through her skull and sprayed the adjacent wall with blood and brains. Her lifeless body fell forward and thumped upon the table. Dan yelped and scrambled to his feet as blood gushed from the wound. A red pool crept across the surface.

Screams ripped through the air as chaos consumed the pub.

Most fled, but some rushed to help.

Dan stood over the table, paralyzed. He gawked at the body in disbelief as random people scurried around him. They asked what happened. They asked if he was okay. They pleaded for answers, but he gave them none, for his focus had shifted to a single, all-consuming observation: a sudden sore throat.

* * *

Inside an emerald-green room, an alien female was asleep inside a transparent cocoon. The oval pod was magnetically suspended and filled with a hazy liquid. She was a slender being with a lean frame and defined muscles. Hygienic light reflected off her hairless skin, highlighting the ribbon-like pattern that painted her from head to toe. Her elongated skull was dotted with dark blue freckles. Thin slits denoted eyes, nostrils, and a mouth. They remained tightly closed, like a slumbering creature from the deep.

A sharp ping echoed inside the room, prompting the pod to float down to the floor. It folded open like a seed pod, spilling its contents across the floor. The casing dissolved and the wash of hazy liquid vanished through a network of drains, leaving the glistening alien lying atop the hard surface. Her nostril slits peeled open to inhale the sterile air. The mouth followed, allowing a thin orange tongue to poke between the lips. Her eyelids blinked open, revealing sapphire irises that swam in a sea of black.

A harsh clank caught her attention.

Her head cocked towards a ray of light that appeared behind her. A pair of similar aliens strolled through the door, each cloaked in form-fitting garb with open arms. One carried a handheld device and the other carried a thin robe. The first alien knelt beside her and pressed the device to her shoulder. It pinged with confirmation and the alien grunt-nodded. The second alien gently assisted her off the floor and into the robe.

"Thank you," she said in their language, but with Julia's voice.

"Welcome back," the assistant said.

"Transfer complete," the scientist said. "All functions stable."

The surveyor nodded her thanks.

The scientist bowed and took his leave.

"Good to be back," she said to the assistant.

"How did it go?"

"Same as Jinthu and Balazec. The core culture is too rapacious. *Was*, rather. I think we dodged another Varokin Crisis."

"That's a shame. They seemed to carry promise."

The surveyor sighed. "Just another example of pushing forward without purging the rot. They haven't even cured cancer, for pity's sake. I mean, the kelp is *right there*."

"A dodge indeed. So where to next?"

"First things first, I need a bite to eat."

"I hear the cafeteria procured some nifku."

"That sounds *perfect*. Lead the way."

They exited the room and the door slid shut. Another sharp ping echoed inside the chamber. An adjacent door slid open, releasing a team of cleaning robots. They dove into work and prepped the room for the next survey.

THE END

Salvation is a key soaked in carnage.

Claymore is a den of monsters, but Vince isn't one of them. He lost everything to a tragic accident, and the years behind bars have tested his will. The world left him to rot. But then he receives a mysterious visitor, who offers a reckoning.

THE CLAYMORE INCIDENT

Claymore housed the worst of the worst. Located inside a mountain gorge and flanked by military forts, the prison was the epitome of maximum security. Its notorious residents were known throughout the world. From serial killers to war criminals, the names within its walls were destined for the history books.

Some, however, were victims of circumstance.

Vince was a mild-mannered chap with a tragic past. He was a building inspector who led a normal life, but a series of unfortunate events found him liable for a structural collapse, killing 36 people. It was a freak accident that no inspector would have caught, but the jury didn't see it that way. Given his record, he should have ended up at a correctional resort. But given the death count, he ended up at Claymore.

Seventeen years after the verdict, Vince remained at Claymore, serving a life sentence for what amounted to a reasonable sign-off. The first years were hard, the next years were suicidal, but then he found peace inside the abyss. He made friends, albeit ones of necessity. The guards liked him and he maintained a perfect behavioral record. He even enjoyed the occasional candy bar smuggled in by those sympathetic to his plight. Now firmly middle-aged, he often wondered when death would come. But in the meantime, he made the best of the predicament by reading, studying, and amassing an impressive number of educational degrees.

Visiting hours were fast approaching and the cellblock was stirring. Vince was sitting at his desk, as usual, taking notes from a textbook. Over the years, he had converted his tiny cell into a modest study. The warden had permitted some bins and bookshelves, as Vince was no more of a threat than the mice that scurried about. He looked forward to visitation because it afforded him some much-needed silence. If he was stuck on a vexing problem, this was precious time to work through it.

The entry door to the block clunked and whined open, but Vince did not react. He merely tidied his notes and prepped his desk for an extended work session. His pencils were sharp, his notepad was fresh, and his brain was ready for a challenge.

"Visitation list," a guard said from afar, part one of a reliable routine.

"Hurry it up, Karl," Vince mumbled to himself. He liked Karl, but the guard took his merry time when it came to visitation. Always by the book.

"94378, Westmore," Karl said.

Ah yes, Billy Westmore. He arrived at Claymore three years ago and his wife visited every week. This week was no different, and the only question was the revealing dress she chose. Billy liked to describe it in detail, which created numerous fantasies for his fellow inmates. She was utterly devoted to him and convinced of his innocence. A lucky man for sure, but also guilty as hell. The visits would continue for a long time to come.

And off he went.

"67612, Grants," Karl said.

Good ol' Reggie Grants. If there was anyone else who didn't belong in Claymore, it was Reggie. The poor guy got a raw deal from a zealous prosecutor. Definitely guilty, but a classic case of the wrong type of person in the wrong type of court. The deck was stacked against him from day one, and he paid the price. His elder mother visited once a month, and it was anyone's guess how long that would last.

And off he went.

"84332, Barrow," Karl said.

Vince scoffed and rolled his eyes. "Not funny, Karl," he said loudly.

"Not joking, Vince. You have a visitor. Stand up and assume the position."

Vince was stunned silent. His lungs swelled and the pencil fell from his hand. He hadn't had a visitor in over a decade. Even his lawyer stopped coming. This had to be a mistake. But on the other hand, it was a rare opportunity to change the scenery. Vince emerged from the daze and shot to his feet, scraping the chair across the concrete floor. He hurried over to the cell door, turned around, and pushed his hands through the tray slot. Jerome, another guard who treated him kindly, cuffed his wrists and motioned for the door to unlock. It did so with a harsh clank, then slid open. Vince spun around and met Jerome with a baffled expression.

"Is this for real?" he said softly.

"As real as a heart attack."

"Who do you think it is?" Vince stepped into the hallway.

Jerome shrugged. "Let's go find out." He nudged Vince's shoulder and escorted him out of the cellblock.

The path to visitation had faded from memory. Vince gazed into the checkpoint booths and guard stations as he passed, unable to link them to previous visits. There was a sterility and hollowness to the journey, but that was true no matter where he went. He remained a blue jumpsuit inside a bleached laboratory. Hard tiles, metal bars, concrete blocks, infinite shades of gray. It was a brutalist's wet dream. Footsteps echoed through the complex like hammer strikes. Locks and latches tore through the air like gunshots. Senses were assaulted in the hollow bowels of Claymore. But then again, comfort was never a priority.

Vince and Jerome arrived at a large holding area outside of visitation. All other cellblocks funneled into the space, creating a bottleneck of access. The open area was three stories tall with observation towers built into the walls, four in total. Bulletproof glass shielded guards as they tended to the control boards. Exterior walkways with blast panels connected the towers. The entire structure loomed over the space like a four-eyed monster. It was a planned chokepoint, should any prisoner harbor delusions of escape.

Some have tried.

All have perished.

A dozen inmates stood inside the holding area with their assigned guards. Vince had no idea if that was a lot. It seemed sparse. But then again, the cavernous space they occupied was most unsettling, no doubt to smother hope. They all faced an oversized door that led to the visitation area. No windows, no handles, no features of any kind. It looked more like the entry to a bank vault. The tower guards finished their security checks, then the door unlocked with a series of harsh clanks. It rumbled atop a rail system and crept into the wall.

And there it was, their only connection to the outside world.

They stared into a long corridor that stretched into the distance. Bulletproof glass lined each wall from floor to ceiling, for obvious reasons. In a crisis situation, visibility was key. Numerous security doors led to various parts of the complex, everything from the armory to the warden's office. The inmates would see none of it, as the first door on the left was the entry to visitation.

A chime echoed overhead, signaling the start of visiting hours. The group shuffled forward and merged into a single line inside the corridor. Once beyond the port, they halted in wait as the security door rumbled shut. A stark meeting area revealed itself through the glass. Twenty metal tables were divided into four rows of five, suitably spaced to avoid intermingling. Metal benches flanked each table and the entire set was welded to the floor.

A dozen tables were occupied. Some were spouses. Others were parents or siblings. A few suits conveyed lawyers and the like. Many waved and smiled as they met their loved ones' gazes through the glass. Vince eyed each of them, but none stared back. The wait was agonizing, even after a decade.

Another chime echoed overhead and the entry door unlocked. One by one, the guards escorted their assigned inmates into the room. Vince and Jerome were near the back. Vince craned his head like an impatient kid at a theme park. The guards delivered their packages, secured them as needed, then stationed themselves along the rear walls.

Vince assessed each delivery.

Spouses taken.

Families taken.

Both suits taken.

But then, near the back, a young woman met his gaze.

She offered Vince an assured smile as he approached. She was in her 30s, by his estimate. Curly red hair, freckles, average build, fairly normal all around. She could have easily been his daughter at this point in his life. And perhaps most puzzling, she wore a stylish summer dress, as if on her way to the beach.

And sure enough, Jerome delivered him directly to her.

Vince gawked at the woman as Jerome uncuffed his hands.

She stood and opened her arms. "My sweet Vince," she said, then stepped forward and wrapped her arms around his neck.

Vince completed the embrace, albeit loosely and with mounting confusion.

Jerome tapped the woman's shoulder. "That's one. You get another at the end. No touching from here on out."

"Yes sir," she said with an upbeat tone. She pulled away and reclaimed her seat.

Jerome smirked at Vince. "Enjoy." He patted Vince's shoulder, then took his leave to claim an assigned station along the rear wall.

Vince, on the contrary, remained stupefied. He stood there motionless, as if awaiting the punchline of a cruel joke.

"Please have a seat," she said, motioning to the other side.

After a brief hesitation, Vince lowered himself onto the bench.

An awkward silence settled between them.

The woman smiled with anticipation, but dared not break the ice.

She left it to Vince, who was more than happy to oblige after a few tense seconds.

"Who are you?" he said.

"I'm your great aunt Gertrude, *obviously*."

Vince cocked an eyebrow. "Well, um, I haven't seen Gerty since my teenage years, but I do know that she would be in her 80s right now."

"Well drat, you caught me," the woman said with a mocking tone, then gestured at the guards along the wall. "*They* didn't, though. The most secure prison in the world and I get in posing as a granny. I did the paperwork and everything. Had my story straight. Thought they'd at least ask me a few questions. Nope. Just flashed a fake ID and got rubber-stamped." She huffed and shook her head. "To be fair, they never look at dates or numbers, just names and pictures. But I'm still weirdly disappointed."

Vince glanced at Jerome, which the woman noticed.

"You wanna tell him?" she said.

"I should."

"But you won't."

"What makes you so sure?"

"Because you haven't seen the inside of this room for 11 years, six months, and two days."

Vince stammered in response.

"And that was your lawyer. He made the trip out here just to tell you in person that there was nothing else he could do. 'I suck at my job and you're trapped here forever. Bye-bye now.' What a douche. And that was two years after your mother stopped coming. Your brother never visited. And he's the one who convinced your mother to snuff out the candle. Your entire family decided to sweep you under the rug. They're doing fine, by the way."

"How do you—"

"You're not going to rat me out because you're lost. You've been abandoned, Vince. Intrigue is the only thing you have left."

Vince eyed Jerome again, but didn't move his head. The hook was in, and his mind slipped into a deep well of mystery. How thin the veneer was between fear and curiosity. He squirmed on the bench and took a deep breath. "So who are you?"

"Nell."

"That's it?"

"What more do you want? I'm a Capricorn and like long walks on the beach. But more to the point, I'm your new best friend."

"That's a leap. I know nothing about you."

"All the reason to chat with me then."

Vince lowered his gaze to the metal surface, trying to make any sense of the situation. The sterile light reflected off the stainless steel, needling his conscience. "So what do you want with me? Why are you here?"

Nell leaned forward. "Vince, my precious little gumdrop, I'm about to make you the most famous person on the planet."

He paused to digest the statement. "Um ... *what?*"

"Seriously. You see these cameras?" She eyed the black domes along the ceiling. "They are about to witness something never before seen in the history of humanity. What we do right now, at this very table, will be studied for centuries." She fanned her fingers, tapped an elbow, and flicked her nose. "Go ahead, do something weird. Anything."

Still confused, Vince lightly thumped his chest like a sad gorilla.

"That was perfect," she said with a chuckle. "A hundred years from now, some poor grad student is going to study that footage and draw some really weird conclusions."

Vince snickered. It was all he could do at that point. Sense, it would seem, was wholly unavailable.

"Anyway," she said, "I'm here to kill Roman Lazarev."

Vince flinched, then snort-chuckled. "Funny."

"I'm serious," she said with an unserious tone.

"The Russian warlord? The Butcher of Belarus? *That* guy?"

"Yup."

"Okay." Vince dropped the bemusement and decided to embrace the entertainment. This woman was clearly insane, so he may as well extract an amusing story. Any minute, the prison would realize its mistake and a guard would take her away. He's done nothing wrong. No harm in seeing how deep the delusion went. He sighed, then resumed a good-natured chat. "Lazarev has been in solitary for three years. I live here and I've never seen him. He is locked away in the deepest, darkest dungeon. How do you intend to kill him?"

"By teleporting through that door." She nodded at the giant metal port through the corridor windows.

Vince paused for thought, then leaned in and rested on his elbows. "I'm sorry, did you just say *teleport?*"

"Yes I did. Hence your imminent fame."

"And how on Earth would that make *me* famous?"

"You'll see."

"Okay." Vince smirked and glanced away for a mental reset. Perhaps insane was a touch too light. Bonkers, bananas, gaga, these felt more fitting. But on the flip side, she remained correct about his assessment. This was by far the most interesting thing that had happened to him over the last decade. He was fully committed to the folly. Nothing left to do but enjoy the ride for as long as it lasted. "So why does Lazarev have to die?"

"Great question," she said like a proud therapist. "Because he's gunning for a deal. He has devastating intel on many of the world's most powerful people, one of whom hired me. This isn't a shiv-in-the-shower kind of job. Lazarev is in Claymore isolation, which means he's essentially on the Moon. I'm the one you call as a last resort."

"So what, you work for the President or something? Does he communicate with you through a chip in your brain?"

Nell snort-laughed. "Witty *and* dignified. I like it. But no, not the President, or any other government goon. I work for *real* power."

"Like who?"

"You wouldn't know. Nobody does. But these people have the entire world by the balls. The biggest names in the muck control more wealth than the Fed."

"They must pay well then."

"Oh yes. In fact, this job will be my swan song. Doing something like this in public requires some epic fuck-off cash. I'm about to be worth more than some small countries."

"Congrats, I guess."

"Thank you." She perked and smiled.

"So, about the teleportation thing." Vince had poked a billion holes in the logic, but couldn't bring himself to pop the bubble. He was enjoying the exchange, as loony as it was. But the ride was coming to an end, and it was time for a soft landing. "If you have that kind of power, then why are you sitting here? Why not blink in from the outside? You can jump directly into his cell and be done with it."

"That's not how it works. Basic physics still applies."

"Of course," Vince said with a bit of snark. He leaned back and crossed his arms. "So what, you got a *Star Trek* teleporter in your pocket?"

"Nope, just me."

"So this is a supernatural thing."

"In a way, but not really."

"That's not as convincing as you think it is."

Nell shrugged and smiled. "I can't just fly through the air or port through a wall. You're thinking of Superman."

"Or Nightcrawler."

"Ah!" She pointed at Vince.

They indulged in a touchless high-five, sharing a moment of fandom respect.

"But no," she continued, "I'm more like The Flash."

"So it's a speed thing."

"Kinda. Yes and no."

Vince laughed, undone by the absurdity.

"I don't know how else to explain it," she said, matching his laugh. "I can move through space instantaneously. Call it a speed thing, call it a teleportation thing, call it a supernatural witch thing."

"So now you're the Scarlet Witch."

"No, smartass." Her chuckles ended with a heavy sigh. "I need a clear visual path, something that exists within the natural physical limits. Basically, if I can walk there, I can teleport there. Those are the rules." Her focus shifted to the giant security gate. "Which means, I need a path through *that* door. And for *that* to happen, the door to visitation must be open too. Two doors, two locks, one magic moment. That's why I'm here with you. I need an event so shocking, so disruptive, that it mobilizes the entire security force. I need chaos. And most importantly, I need victims."

Vince shrank away as a grim tension infected the table.

Sensing the unease, she snapped back to a bubbly persona. "No need to worry, though. You did me a huge solid by getting me here. You're good people, Vince. I'm not going to touch one hair on that slightly balding head."

Vince scrunched his brow and patted his scalp. He had forgotten what a polite tease felt like. It was strangely pleasant, so he opted for some self-deprecation to soften the vibe. "Good people, huh? The fine citizens of my jury beg to differ."

"Nah, I read your profile. You were done dirty. In fact, that's why I chose you. If anyone in this pit deserves a second chance, it's you."

"You read my story?" he said with a half-smile. A strange sensation tingled inside his chest. It was foreign yet familiar, a token from the distant past. Someone had taken a genuine interest in his life. A dark cloud had followed Vince ever since his lawyer threw in the towel. It broke his spirit, but a ray of light had finally poked through. It warmed the table and gifted him a moment of gratitude. "Thank you," he said, and actually meant it. He took a measured breath, then folded his arms on the table. "So what's the play here, Ms. Teleporter?"

She smirked. "You still don't believe me, do you?"

Vince shrugged. "What can I say? It's a bit much."

Nell pursed her lips and feigned disgust. "After all we've been through, you don't believe a word I've said."

"Don't get me wrong, you're a very interesting young lady. And you're right, I don't have the slightest beef with how you got here. You've actually been a breath of fresh air, despite your kooky claims."

"Kooky? Kind Mr. Vincent, I will have you know that teleportation, and my mastery of it, are firmly rooted in the cold, hard foundation of reality."

"Okay. Then prove it."

She cocked an eyebrow. "What do you have in mind?"

"Beats me. Swipe a guard's badge or something."

She nodded in thought, then grunted. "I have a better idea. But you have to do something for me first."

"That was a quick cop out."

"Nah nah nah, it's not like that." She glanced around the room for a moment, then leaned in with a muted voice. "Who in here is the biggest piece of shit?"

"Come again?"

"You know, the pedos, the wife-beaters, the scum of humanity. Who in here would make the world a better place if they didn't exist?"

Vince pondered the question, then pulled his gaze around the room. After a quick survey, he nodded towards a nearby meathead. "That guy. Paulie. Let's just say that he likes 'em a bit too young. Most of us deserve to be here, but those types need to be *under* the prison. Monsters like him usually get a proper comeuppance within these walls. But as you can see, Paulie is big enough that no one ever messes with him."

Nell donned a toothy grin. "He's perfect."

"So what, you gonna teleport a spanking?"

"Not exactly." She gave Paulie a long, hard stare. "You know what's interesting about teleportation?" Her gaze floated back to Vince, who recoiled with an unexpected fright. The whites of her eyes had turned black and her irises pulsed with a haunting blue charge. "Some truly fascinating things happen to the physical world in that moment," she continued. "Fabric tears apart like tissue paper. Flesh becomes viscous, like molasses. I can reach into someone's ribcage and pop their heart like a ripe tomato." A menacing grin crept across her face. "But do you know what holds up surprisingly well?"

Vince stammered, but then a sudden shift in Nell's posture rendered him silent. It was a snap in time, a glitch, like a missing frame in a film reel. She was naked. Her summer dress had been torn to shreds and bits of fabric rested on the table. Her grin remained, but her face and bare chest were speckled with blood. His widened eyes detached from her blackened stare and lowered to the femur bone that she held aloft between them. It glistened with a red sheen that soaked her hand and dripped onto the table. Bits of flesh and tendon were still attached. She lowered it to the surface and let it rest like a grisly trophy.

A shriek tore through the room.

Vince flinched and whipped his horrified gaze to the source. Paulie wailed in unspeakable pain as a giant gash in his thigh gushed blood onto the floor. The flesh was limp and elastic, like an empty rubber tube. Paulie clawed at the gaping wound as the entire room leapt to its feet in terror. Many screamed with him, but none rushed to help. The guards remained pinned to the walls, their eyes wide with shock. Paulie's brother remained frozen at the table, gawking at the gash with his mouth agape.

Vince whipped his gaze back to Nell.

She raised a bloody palm, motioning to stay put. "Let it play out," she said, her black eyes still awash in blue static.

Vince trembled as his mind struggled to grasp the new reality.

"Like I said," she continued, "you're about to become one of the most famous people to have ever lived. I only ask that you do one thing for me in return."

Vince nodded.

Nell smiled, then rose to her feet and walked to his side of the table. She leaned down and whispered into his ear. The exchange was brief, but decisive. She leaned back and met his gaze one last time. "Can you do that for me?"

Vince nodded again.

"Good." She patted his shoulder, then grabbed the femur bone off the table and turned to the commotion. The wails and screams continued, filling the space with an echo of panic. Most had fled to the walls. Some hid under the tables. The guards had inched forward with batons drawn, but dared not confront the devil. Nell met their gazes through a darkened void, infecting the space with a dreadful anticipation. As if on cue, an alarm blared through the intercom system. Nell rolled her shoulders and tightened her grip. "And here we go."

Every voice ceased with a deafening pop, leaving only the siren.

Vince, now caked in flesh and blood, shivered with fright as his widened eyes surveyed a gory aftermath. Skulls were exploded. Ribs were splintered. Limbs were ripped from sockets. Every human body was obliterated. A thick red goop trickled down the walls and dripped from the ceiling. The carnage was ferocious and absolute.

And there, standing in the middle, was Nell.

Blood soaked her naked body from head to toe. Bits of flesh fell from her hair, now sodden with a meaty soup. Clutched in her hands were two femur bones. One from Paulie, and another from a mystery donor. She stared at the glass corridor with her back to Vince. A chorus in the distance swelled with commanding voices and tromping boots. They merged with the blaring siren, creating the harshest of melodies.

Nell glanced over her shoulder. "Remember what I said."

Vince nodded again, unable to speak.

The main security door rumbled open, stealing Nell's attention. Armed guards poured into the corridor. Their shock was instant and apparent, for a demon had entered their domain. They met her black eyes through the observation windows, but Nell did not react. She merely waited for the moment. That perfect, precise, unmistakable moment.

One of the guards unlocked the visitation door.

He and another flowed into space with rifles raised.

Nell grinned, then vanished with another deafening pop.

Fountains of blood painted the corridor red, and a string of mangled corpses crumpled to the floor.

For the first time in 17 years, Vince was alone. Truly alone. The ensuing slaughter echoed from deep inside the complex. Screams, panic, gunfire, and then a cold silence. He knew that Nell had completed her mission. Dripping blood filled the void, drawing his attention back to the table. Vince remained seated, as if chained to the floor and unable to accept his freedom. But a god among the damned had given him a task, and fear would see it done. And so he sat there, caked in carnage, treading water in a lake of death.

* * *

A full hour had passed before another guard entered the visitation area. He came through the bloodied entry with a rifle raised and several more guards in tow. Body armor encased him from head to toe.

Not a guard.

Something else.

Special ops, likely from the military fort.

The soldier quickly scanned the room and locked onto Vince, who was still sitting at the table with his hands resting on the surface. His palms were flat and his fingers were spread to convey compliance. The gruesome scene and unnerving calm painted Vince as a serial killer reveling in his work. But a killer he was not. He was merely a pawn in a fiendish game. The soldier pushed forward with intent. He motioned to the others, who broke away to secure the room. The soldier halted at the table with his rifle aimed at Vince's head.

"Identify yourself," the soldier said with a stern voice.

"Vincent Barrow," he said. "Inmate 84332."

"Where is she?"

Vince glanced around the room one last time. He took a deep breath, filling his lungs with a lingering stench of iron. His eyes lifted to the soldier and met his gaze through the helmet visor. "I cannot say. But I do have a message for your commanding officer."

* * *

Two weeks later, Vince was sitting at a large conference table in Washington, D.C. He wore a pinstripe suit with a blue tie and black dress shoes. His hands were folded atop the polished oak surface, a far cry from his tiny prison desk. He was alone on his side of the table, but on the other sat a four-star general and several members of the Joint Chiefs of Staff.

A heavy silence lingered between them.

They had just screened the security footage of Nell's rampage through Claymore, the first time Vince had seen it. She had torn through personnel like a blade through grass. It was a hell of a thing to watch a blood-soaked naked woman massacre a prison with a pair of femur bones. When she reached Lazarev, she dropped her weapons, gripped the bars of the cell door, and pulsed it off the rails with a static surge. The door sizzled with a blue charge as it crashed to the ground, leaving nothing between Nell and her prize. Lazarev was pressed to the rear wall, his palms raised and eyes wide with terror. He uttered a single word of an impassioned plea before Nell blinked forward and popped his head like a water balloon. His lifeless body slumped to the floor, leaving a large red flower painted on the wall. Nell turned to face the camera and the feed ended on a still frame.

Vince stared at the laptop screen across the table, gazing into her black eyes once again. He could feel her staring back, demanding her penance.

Remember what I said.

All eyes were locked on Vince with cautious intrigue.

One of the officials placed his hand atop a leatherbound folder and slid it to the center of the table. Vince eyed it for a moment, then reached over and pulled the folder to his side. He glanced down to see the glimmer of a White House seal. A surreal moment, but also one of triumph and perseverance. With a slow and steady hand, he opened the cover to reveal the ultimate prize. It was merely a dream not weeks before, but there it was.

A full presidential pardon.

"Is it done then?" he said to the group, but did not lift his gaze.

"Yes," an official said, "with the full understanding of your recip-rocation."

Vince nodded.

"To recap," another official said, checking her notes, "an unidentified woman entered—"

"Nell," Vince said as he lifted his head.

"Excuse me?"

"Her name was Nell."

"Nell what?"

"I don't know."

"Then how is it relevant?"

Vince shrugged. "Just thought you would like to know."

The general shifted in his chair, clearly losing patience.

"Anyway," the official continued, "an unidentified woman, Nell, entered the Claymore Correctional Facility posing as your aunt."

"Great aunt."

The official sneered across the table.

Vince waved off the blunder. "Sorry."

"You engaged in a conversation in the visitation area, much of which has been translated through the available surveillance footage. You reviewed the transcript. Do you deny any of its contents?"

"No."

"She then proceeded to murder 46 guards, 18 civilians, and 11 inmates to reach Roman Lazarev, whom she assassinated before vanishing without a trace. She accomplished this by means of a ... *unique* ability, hitherto unknown. Do you dispute any of this?"

"No."

"Shortly before infiltrating the primary facility, she relayed a message to you. It was strategically hidden to thwart surveillance. She then—"

"What did she tell you?" the general said with a gravelly voice.

A tense silence enveloped the space.

Vince smiled and nodded, the first time he showed any real emotion since the incident. He took a needed breath, then leaned forward and locked eyes with the general.

The entire group matched the lean.

"She said ..." Vince paused to savor the moment. *Enjoy the fame. Use it to get out of here and milk it for all it's worth.* "Your story is one of many. Help them. And tell the brass that I'm watching."

The general ruffled his brow, then turned a troubled look to one of the staff. The officials squirmed in their chairs, realizing that a brutal upheaval was imminent. The era of corporate incarceration had come to an end with a harrowing declaration. It landed on the table like an anvil and shook the very foundation of the justice system.

Vince stood from the table, grabbed the folder, and tucked it under his shoulder. Facing the group, he said, "I have spent 17 years in Claymore. My crime was a hapless accident. Even the judge acknowledged it. 'A black swan event,' she said. And yet, I was to spend the rest of my life paying for it in the most notorious prison on the planet. And for what? So families could feel better about a faultless tragedy. There are a lot of Vincent Barrows in the world. Find them. Free them." He pointed at the laptop across the table. "Or face her."

An empty threat, but they didn't know that.

Vince turned away and walked towards the exit. His footsteps echoed like hammer strikes, pounding a sudden dread that befell the group. A smirk puckered his cheeks as he relished the sweet taste of vindication. He pushed through the double doors and vanished into the hall as a free and exonerated man.

The footage had leaked online, and the world was enraptured by the mystery woman. The press had dubbed it The Claymore Incident, and a tidal wave of conspiracy theories had already taken root. And Vince, being the sole survivor, had indeed become the most famous person on the planet. A whirlwind of intrigue surrounded him and the press was hungry for their scoops. They awaited him outside. All of them, from every corner of the globe. The entire planet was breathless with anticipation. Vince, now the most seductive persona of his generation, and for many generations to come, was more than happy to give them what they wanted.

For a price.

THE END

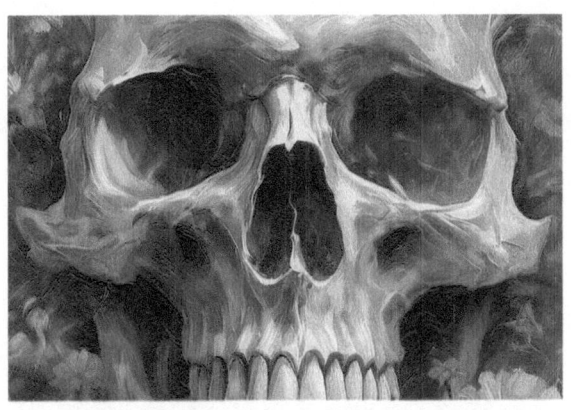

Peace is the ultimate ruin of power.

Ishuun is a planet forged in war. After ages of bloodshed, a lone orphan rises from the chaos to unite the nations. His grandson, Noros, inherits the throne and brings lasting peace. But in the silence that follows, a lurking madness begins to stir.

NOROS

The nations of Ishuun warred for thousands of years. The planet was located in dead space, an area deemed too remote for Federation interest. It matured into an advanced civilization, but one wholly disconnected from the greater cosmos. As the technology grew, so did the conflicts. Power struggles dominated the globe. Factions rose and fell inside a perpetual war that claimed countless lives over millennia.

Rulers came and went. Each declared a grand solution, and each faced a tribunal for heinous crimes. But then, a nameless orphan rose through the ranks to establish an ethical bond with the greater population. He united a few factions, restored their pride, then united some more. Under a banner of peace and prosperity, he mollified half the planet before he died. His daughter united the next quarter, and her son was tasked to unite the rest.

His name was Noros.

* * *

The palace was quiet that day, a most auspicious day. A team of curators had stripped the throne room of unnecessary frills, leaving only a series of banners along the central walkway. Their shimmering black fabric featured national crests with silver stitching. Seventeen in total, all hanging from mighty pillars that flanked the path from entry to throne. They represented the triumphant resolutions of long and brutal conflicts.

An eerie stillness infected the space.

Lighting domes around the room had dimmed for the occasion, save for the throne and pillars. The ceiling was black and distant, creating the illusion that the banners were hanging from the darkness itself. The throne was a towering structure carved from white marble. Its slender frame and slanted peak resembled the blade of a knife. It rested on a platform of black stone, which stood a meter high with wide steps carved into the face. Contrasted with the gray stone of the cavernous room, it served as a visual shock.

Several sentries stood at the base, each cocooned in black armor. They gripped silver glaives with glowing blue blades, the feared weapon of the palace guard. They emitted trails of crackling energy when swung. The harrowing image spawned numerous stories of guards besting foes like bedeviled ghosts. And given their unparalleled skill, such stories were not unfounded.

The core council had gathered atop the platform and flanked the throne. Advisors wore silver robes with white veils, representing the high priests of old. Mireth, the second in command, wore a fitted black suit with a distinct lack of flair. Her dark presence created the image of a would-be assassin, but a threat she was not. The power she wielded dwarfed all but one. She stood beside the throne with arms locked behind her back.

Noros sat upon the throne with hands folded in his lap. His posture was stiff and forward, as if to receive a secret. Black fabric wrapped his body in a complex weave, a feat accomplished by a team of trained professionals. Silver chains hung from his neck and attached to an emblem that rested on his chest. Numerous jewels adorned his wrists and fingers, but none were garish to the point of distraction. The emblem was the focus, depicting an all-seeing eye that rested inside a cupped palm. Only one person was permitted to wear the image, and that person was the emperor.

A rush of static broke the stillness.

All eyes turned to the circular receiving area at the base of the platform, where a hologram image began to assemble. The bust of a woman formed from the ether. She wore crisscrossed sashes with a pin atop her chest, signifying rank. A simple cap with a palace seal completed the picture of a devoted deputy.

"They're here," she said.

Noros inhaled a measured breath, then nodded. "Send them in."

A harsh clunk echoed around the room. The mighty entry doors whined open, compelled by powerful magnetic strips embedded in the floor. A pool of light spilled into the room, tracing the shadows of five visitors. The doors pushed to the walls and the whines ceased.

Silence returned for a moment.

It was the last moment of its kind, broken by heels on stone.

The five figures approached the throne in unison, all cloaked in crimson robes. The woman in front had her face and arms exposed, but the others were veiled entirely. Simple brown cords encircled their waists, giving them a hallowed appearance. The woman carried a wooden staff and one of the figures carried a small chest. The rest bore nothing, but this was expected. Forged weaponry was forbidden in their order. Their acumen was elemental magic, a formidable power that made them a potent adversary.

The woman glanced at the banners as she approached, but showed little emotion. She maintained a steady pace from the entry to the receiving circle, where she and the other four marched to a stop.

"Emperor Noros," she said, not wasting time.

"Queen Raenatha," he said. "Thank you for making the journey."

"Thank you for receiving us." She offered a slight nod.

Noros stood from the throne, drawing the gazes of everyone present. A sudden tension infected the space as he stepped forward and slowly descended the platform. The nearest guard turned his head to offer support, but Noros waved it away with a subtle gesture. He took a final step into the receiving circle, bringing him and the

Red Queen face-to-face. An air of familiarity seemed to abate the lingering tension. They exchanged polite smiles.

"Raena," he said.

"Nori," she said.

"It's been a long time since our days in the palace."

"That it has. I passed the gardens where we used to play. Still looks the same."

Noros grinned. "The council does have a penchant for tradition." He glanced over his shoulder. "I mean, look at them. They're dressed like thousand-year-old priests who think the suns are chariots."

Raena snort-chuckled.

"Good to hear that laugh again. In any context."

She nodded in solidarity, then resumed a cold demeanor. She motioned to the veiled figure behind her, who stepped to her side and presented the small wooden chest. The queen unlatched the lid and lifted it open to reveal a golden sceptre tucked into a crimson cloth. At the top, a red jewel was grasped by two talons, the symbol of their order. She lifted it from the enclosure and presented it to the emperor with both hands at the poles.

Noros reached forward and gripped the center.

She met his gaze and said, "With this gift, The Order of Filandra accepts unification." She released her grip and withdrew her arms, leaving Noros with the sceptre.

Silence returned to the throne room.

Noros stared at the sceptre in his hand as an unexpected sensation consumed him. It was a deep fissure, a scream in the dark. His heart began to race as his lungs swelled with dread. The guards tightened their grips on the glaives as they watched the sceptre tremble in the emperor's hand. Tensions mounted as his widened eyes lifted to the queen. He struggled to find the words and stammered with confusion.

"Noros, what's wrong?" she said with genuine concern.

"Excuse me," he said, then turned away and hurried around the platform.

As he vanished from sight, Mireth detached from her position and lunged forward. Sensing the unrest, she gestured a subtle apology as she descended the platform steps. Without a word, she scurried after Noros and slipped into the dark.

After a brief search, she found him inside the council chamber, a shielded meeting area behind the throne. He stood at the rear glass panes that overlooked the city. The sceptre was pressed to his chest as he stared into the depths. The palace was the tallest structure in a vast ocean of steel. Countless other towers rose from its glowing blue foundation, the churning heart of a sprawling metropolis. He watched shuttles and cruisers glide upon invisible lanes, creating veins of traffic that resembled cells in a bloodstream.

Mireth settled beside him without a word.

"Is this real?" he said with a muted voice.

"World peace," she said, matching the tone. "Actual world peace. You have just achieved something that no one thought possible, on this world or any other."

"My grandfather was right."

"And your mother would be proud."

His gaze lowered to the sceptre. "I guess it had to be Raena."

"Kind of poetic, if you ask me."

"How so?"

"You were best friends. She left the palace, chose a path, and became an enemy. This city represents the antithesis of her order. And yet, she came back. She is the leader of the last rebel nation, and she came back. She doesn't fear *us*. She trusts *you*. We all do."

Noros sighed and nodded. "Thank you, Mireth."

"You're welcome." She turned to face him, then gestured towards the throne room. "That said, trust is fleeting. Best not to keep them waiting."

He grinned. "Right. Lead the way."

* * *

The announcement was aired that day and the world united in celebration. Noros gave an impassioned speech and the press crowned him The Peacemaker. A torrent of fawning pieces was published through the live wires. World peace had been achieved, they all exclaimed. A solid week of jubilation turned into a new normal, an entire planet beyond war and bloodshed. Pacts were written. Trade was enshrined. There was an immediate and zealous reaction to protect the new world order. Noros was deified in the minds of the people. He was the best among them, and the planet was unified in its adoration.

But the veneration would take its toll.

Noros, weary of the ceaseless praise, withdrew from the public eye. He retreated deep into the palace, far from doting staff and prying questions. A seldom-used wing became his refuge, where he spent time reading history books and scribbling thoughts. Weeks turned into months, and months turned into a curious public. Only Mireth was permitted to visit. She assumed the role of caretaker, both of him and the throne.

* * *

The wing was dimly lit, as always. Noros preferred the dark. He said it cleared the mind by bringing important queries into focus. Mireth played along, but the entry corridor always put her nerves on edge. The heels of her boots clacked upon the stone, sending sharp echoes through the passage. A gray shawl had replaced her black uniform, giving her a more casual appearance. She carried a pair of beverages in silver mugs. Ribbons of steam snaked over the rims and vanished into the darkness.

A pair of wall sconces signaled the end of the passage. They emitted a blue glow and flanked a large wooden door with black rivets. She strolled to a stop and leaned towards a small panel embedded in the frame. The facial scanner confirmed her presence. A chime sounded and the door unlocked, allowing her to push it open with a firm shoulder. Once inside, the door whined shut and relatched.

Mireth paused inside a small chamber, also dimly lit with blue sconces. Two doors, one to either side, led to a bedroom and a storage facility. On the far wall was a large fire pit with an ornate hearth. Embers crackled beneath an ebbing flame. A pair of lounge chairs flanked the pit, one of which was occupied by Noros. A thick robe covered his body, leaving only his stubbled face to the withering light. He stared at the embers with an emptiness, lost in thought, oblivious to the presence of another.

Mireth sighed, then continued her walk towards the pit. She set the mugs on a small table between the chairs and claimed the other seat. Her body sank into the plush material, drawing a sigh of contentment. The comfort was brief, as her continued meetings with Noros had achieved very little. He devolved into a stamp, a bleak and distant nod that kept the world turning. Mireth was capable, but a leader she was not, and her patience was wearing thin.

"Drink," she said with a firm tone.

Noros complied, albeit loosely and without much regard.

"Where are you today?" she said.

"Same," he said somberly. "A remote void somewhere in the stars."

"Any plans on coming back?"

Noros did not respond.

"The council is making plans," she continued. "There will be an event on the one-year anniversary of the final pledge. We need to show the world that our stability is absolute. This needs to be an ongoing pledge that we return to the people, and they need to believe it."

Noros did not respond, prompting Mireth to lean forward and clap loudly at him. Noros flinched and barked back. "What the hell are you—"

"Shut the fuck up and listen." Her face was taut with anger, as the last sliver of patience had worn away. "I have no idea what has gotten into you, and at this point, I don't care. This is the beginning of a rarefied era, something that civilizations can only dream of. I am not going to let *you* take that away from *them*. Lead what you have earned, or we will find someone who will." She leaned back into the chair, but her fury remained.

Noros stared at her in disbelief. He could not recall the last time someone spoke to him in that manner, if ever. Threatening the emperor was instant death. Mireth knew that, but she was unafraid. She wasn't a citizen addressing a ruler. She was a concerned friend. Tough love, as they say. Noros glanced at the crackling pit, nodded, then returned his gaze to Mireth.

"Can I pick the decorations?" he said.

Mireth snorted into a smile. "You can fill the room with confetti for all I care. The only thing I want there is *you*."

Noros matched her smile and reached over the table.

She grasped his hand.

"Thank you," he said.

"Fuck you," she said, mockingly.

"I'm sorry I put you through this, but I'm going to make it right."

"You'd better," she said and their hands parted. "Are you ever going to tell me what this was? I should know in case I need to kick you in the shin."

He contemplated the question, then sighed. "In time."

* * *

The day had come for the grand speech and the throne room was awash with gilding. A warm glow filled the space and the ceiling was covered in ceremonial banners. Several drone cameras hovered below them, streaming live images to the entire planet.

Every world leader had converged in the space. All 18 nations were assembled, including the most recent inductee. Raena stood inside the receiving circle, proudly representing the Order of Filandra. Her crimson robe stood out among the rest, all of whom were gathered inside the circle. Some wore stately attire. Others wore ancestral robes to honor history. And on that day, all were serving the United Planet of Ishuun.

Standing behind the leaders was a throng of invited guests. Family, legislators, executives, even a cohort of distinguished citizens. Smiles adorned every face, as no one dared to discount the monumental nature of the moment. They were witnesses, not only to the dream of a planet, but to the dream of the greater cosmos. A new reality, proof of the impossible. They reveled in the prestige and deserved every second.

Noros stood upon the throne platform with the entire council gathered around him. He wore an ornate black uniform with a single silver sash. The emperor's seal rested on his chest. Mireth stood beside him in her usual dark attire and serious stare. The entire palace guard stood around the platform, filling the rear quarter of the throne room. Their matching black armor and polished silver glaives gave them a regal vibe, like pawns on a kingly chessboard.

Noros raised both arms into the air.

The murmuring crowd went silent.

All cameras turned to the throne.

"Not one person on this planet has known peace," he said with a booming voice. "True peace. A world without war. My mother didn't know it. Her father didn't know it. Not a single soul of our collective ancestors knew it. And yet, here we are, basking in a reality no one ever thought possible."

The crowd erupted with applause.

"Eighteen nations have gathered inside this room," he continued. "The whole of Ishuun, and the only foe I see is the fashion coordinator."

A warm chuckle lifted from the mass.

Noros gestured at one of the leaders, a middle-aged man with coiffed hair and a belly shaped by leisure. He was wrapped inside a full set of formal armor that glistened in the bright light. An orange sash draped across his chest with his nation's crest stitched into the fabric.

"Maron of Hivaan," Noros said with a wide smile. "Would you join me at my side?"

The man matched the smile and stepped forward with pride.

"As we all know," Noros said as Maron ascended the platform

steps, "Hivaan was the first nation to accept my grandfather's accord. We shared a border that saw more blood than rain. But every fantasy requires a first step towards reality. And today, my esteemed guest is kind enough to take the final steps."

Maron stepped onto the platform and into a firm handshake, much to the delight of the gathered mass and watchers around the world. They exchanged respectful nods, then parted hands and settled side-by-side facing the crowd.

Noros rested a hand on Maron's shoulder and continued his speech. "From that fateful day, when my grandfather shook the hand of his enemy, Ishuun has been building to this moment." His smile faded as he slowly withdrew his hand. "But I assure you all, it is not the moment you were expecting."

Maron barked with fright as the head of a glaive burst through his chest. A spray of blood rained upon the platform steps. The crowd watched in stunned silence as his body rose into the air. A nameless soldier stood behind him with the glaive pommel planted on the floor. Maron shrieked in pain, prompting numerous screams from the crowd. His arms flailed as his impaled body hovered above the platform. Blood gushed from his chest, crawled down every limb, and spilled onto the cold black stone. The glowing blue blade crackled inside the wound, jolting its helpless victim with surges of energy.

Chaos gripped the room, but only for a moment.

The palace guard pounded their glaives in unison, showing sparks and sending a frightful thunder across the room. A grim silence followed. The front guards lowered their glaives to a readied stance, conveying that any interference would be met with the same fate. Some tried to flee, but all exits had been locked. They were trapped, an enslaved audience to the coming address.

"What you have just witnessed," Noros said with a venomous tone, "was the end of a long and patient coup. Over the last several months, I learned that Hivaan intended to overthrow my rule and install a tyrannical regime in its place." His furious gaze locked onto the nearest camera. "Maron betrayed my grandfather's glorious vision, *our* vision, and sought to deny *your* peace to enrich his own nation."

The aura inside the room suddenly shifted.

Fear, it would seem, was giving way to something far more pernicious.

Noros reached to his side and opened his palm, prompting a soldier to surrender their glaive. He glanced over his shoulder to Mireth, whose widened eyes conveyed shock and horror. Noros did not react. The palace guard was loyal to the emperor. She and the council were trapped by his whim, rooted to their places like cornered prey. Noros turned back to Maron, and with a single mighty swipe, decapitated his foe. The crowd gasped as the head bounced on the platform and rolled to a rest.

A hush fell upon the throne room.

Noros tossed the glaive back to the guard, who caught it with both hands and resumed a readied position. He reached down, grabbed the head of Maron, and walked over to the white throne. Lifting the head with both hands, he smeared the bloody stump across the marble, painting a grisly red stripe across the face. "That," he said, turning to face the crowd, "is the closest Hivaan will ever get to the seat of power."

The crowd remained silent, but a bubbling fury was palpable. Noros pulled his gaze across the gathered mass. The shock had dissipated, and the only surviving fear was Hivaani. One face, however, carried a vicious glare. Raena stared at Noros with utter contempt. Disdain oozed from her body, and Noros knew that she would lead the rebellion. He also knew that he could stifle it right then and there.

But where was the fun in that?

His eyes locked onto the camera as he lifted the head high into the air. "This is what I want from you, brave citizens of Ishuun! Hivaani are the enemies of peace! They are the monsters in the dark, plotting and scheming to steal what is rightfully yours! Take back your planet! Kill every Hivaani and bring their heads to me!"

The crowd roared, sending chills down the spines of every Hivaani.

"Hear me now and hear me well," Noros continued. "I hereby

declare a royal bounty. For every Hivaani head you bring to me, I shall reward you one million marks."

The roars quieted.

Mumbles crept through the mass as a sudden allure set in.

All eyes immediately scanned the crowd.

"For Ishuun!" said a random man, who turned and attacked his neighbor.

The resulting chaos was merciless and absolute. Fitted suits and glittering gowns devolved into the shells of clawing animals. Screams filled the throne room as the first blood of genocide spilled onto the floor.

* * *

The response was ferocious.

Friends murdered friends, family murdered family, entire communities were butchered and looted in the name of peace. Law and order evaporated overnight, save for the central palace, which was fortified for a lengthy siege. Even Noros was impressed by the swiftness of carnage. He expanded the palace guard and barricaded the throne block, where he gave regular goading speeches to a planet soaked in bloodshed.

Decapitated heads flooded the palace steps. The entire population was registered in the Ishuun archives, complete with national and biological markers. A simple verification system was created, which confirmed identities and awarded funds to the carriers. Heads vanished into the palace and newly minted millionaires departed to grow their riches. Bloodlust morphed into headhunter factions, which used fear and intimidation to assume control of local districts. Before long, the global order had crumbled into anarchy.

Hivaan fell as a nation and the citizens fled into hiding. The frail and elderly were rounded up and beheaded for profit. The factions set up checkpoints around the palace and stole heads from anyone seeking reward. Borders were patrolled by rival gangs, which often broke out into violent conflict. Mercenary groups were hired to hunt the remaining Hivaani, which shared profit with the headhunter factions. At least, when advantageous. Many factions were swallowed whole by mercenary invasions.

After one month, the Hivaani ceased to exist as a race. Headhunters drained the palace funds and the global economy was thrown into peril. In response, Noros cooked up another story where Hivaan had secretly aligned with another nation. The fury swelled and the speeches intensified, provoking a cataclysmic response. The cycle repeated and the economy collapsed. Wealth turned to dust and the resource wars began. Nations turned on each other. Brutal civil wars reduced the population to a fraction of its peak. A brutal famine crept across the planet, consuming the weak and weary.

And so was born the rebellion.

Mireth, the ousted second hand of Noros, rose from the ruins of civilization to command a resistance army. The remaining powers banded together with a plan to attack the throne. Raena became their leader. Using her intimate knowledge of Noros, she constructed a counter-narrative to break his spell. They branded him a madman and promised to end the tyranny. Peace would return, but not before the delirium had been vanquished. Noros struck back, spurring his loyalists to sacrifice themselves for the glory of Ishuun.

But the message was dead.

As the rebels pushed towards the capital, the palace guard abandoned Noros and left him to his fate. Mireth and her troops stormed the palace with little resistance. They broke through the gates and worked their way up the tower, slaying anyone who opposed. Few did. Most dropped their arms and pleaded for absolution. The exhaustion was written across their faces. Survival had been their only driving ideal.

Six months after Noros incited a genocide, Raena and Mireth stood outside the throne room. A battalion of troops surrounded them, ready to give their lives to end the madness.

* * *

The lights had dimmed in the entry corridor. Not by choice, but by a failing power grid. Sconces flickered inside the hallway, highlighting a collection of dusty decor that hadn't been cleaned in months. An eerie stillness had gripped the space, an area once bustling with staff and visitors. But there in the darkness stood a new ensemble. Their leader was cloaked in red, and her followers were wrapped in the tattered rags of war.

Mireth studied the giant entry doors to the throne room, their metal faces tarnished with grime and neglect. She motioned to a demolition man, who stepped forward to work his magic. He affixed a device to the seam and armed it with a few knowing flicks. It hummed to life and the man took a few steps back. The seam flashed and several clatters echoed inside the throne room. The man removed the device and nodded at Mireth, signaling that all internal barricades had been destroyed.

She then gestured to a pair of soldiers, who stepped forward and pressed their shoulders into the doors. They pushed in unison and the panes cracked open. The hinges whined as they shoved through debris and into the throne room.

Mireth gasped.

Her stomach twisted as a horrifying vision unfolded. Countless heads were piled inside the throne room. Mountains of flesh and bone rose to either side, rotting away in the unbearable heat. They encircled the pillar bases and vanished into the darkness above. A small path snaked through the gore and up to the throne. A vile and choking aroma flooded the entry hall, forcing the gathered rebels to quell vomits. Many couldn't. A cloud of buzzing flies created a haunting drone, and their ravenous maggots feasted on the carnage.

Mireth turned her attention to the throne.

There, draped across the filthy white marble, was Noros.

"Welcome," he said with a mocking tone.

Mireth did not respond. She gathered her wits, resumed a commanding grace, and stepped forward with a slow and steady pace. Her eyes met the empty gazes of countless faces along the path. All had met their untimely ends at the whim of a maniac. Anger and sorrow swelled in her chest. It clawed at her focus and yearned to escape in a cathartic wail.

So cruel.

So evil.

So ... pointless.

Her gaze detached from the fallen and refocused on Noros, who donned a sly smile as he watched her approach. Following Mireth were several armored rebels and Raena. Her red cloak blended into the gore, but she did not grieve the dead. Her gaze was fixed on the throne. Blood and muck squished beneath their feet as they marched towards cessation.

Mireth reached the end of the grisly path and continued up the platform steps, maintaining eye contact with Noros. A stained silver robe hung loosely around his shoulders. He rested on an elbow with one leg dangling over an armrest. A last stand perhaps, but the lack of fight did little to calm the nerves.

Mireth stepped onto the platform and paused before the throne. She loomed over Noros, casting a shadow across the white marble. The soldiers remained at the base as Raena ascended the steps and settled beside Mireth. Their eyes burrowed into the emperor, one with chagrin, and the other with contempt.

"Would you like some tea?" Noros said in jest.

"You die today," Mireth said. "You know that, right?"

"I surmised."

"Why?" Raena said sharply.

"Come again, love?"

"Maron was innocent. Hivaan was an ally. You knew that. Why?"

Noros paused in thought, then sighed. "Because you made me irrelevant."

Raena and Mireth traded puzzled glances.

"I was a savior," Noros continued, "the collective hope of a war-torn planet. You took that away from me. Nothing kills power quite like peace."

"But you're the one who sought pea—"

"And you accepted it!" he said, snapping back in anger. "I had the faith and fear of a sacred promise. You stole it away and turned me into a token of the past."

Mireth stammered, her voice cracking with dismay. "You murdered half the planet ... to feel needed again?"

Noros grinned. "No one remembers peace and abundance. It's boring. The people yearn for plagues and chaos. They're animals with a death wish, and I'm their king." He snatched a dagger from beneath his robe and thrust it at Mireth.

But she did not flinch.

The blade had stopped within an inch of her chest, trapped inside an unseen field. Noros grimaced as a fiery pain crept down his arm and spread across his body, paralyzing him. He snarled with contempt, for he knew the sorcery that befell him. Raena had sensed the threat and intercepted the strike.

"It had to be you," he said, meeting Raena's gaze.

Her eyes glowed red with elemental power, matching the rage that boiled within. Noros sought a glorious death, but she refused. With a calm and sovereign voice, she said, "Your grandfather died as The Uniter. Your mother died as The Arbiter. Their legacies will inspire generations to come. We will tell their stories, but we will never laud the wicked."

Noros sneered through the pain.

Raena lowered to a knee, bringing them face-to-face. "Your betters constructed the ship and steadied the waters. All you did was sink it in the harbor. Weakness is your legacy, and history is ours to write. And so shall endure the ballad of Noros The Lesser."

She lifted an open palm between them, then slowly curled her fingers inward.

Noros winced in pain as his brain contracted. His entire body twitched and seized. Whimpers erupted into screams as his cerebrum ripped under the pressure. Blood squirted from his eyes and ears. Brain matter oozed from his nose and mouth.

"Goodbye, Noros," Raena said as she clawed her fingers into a fist.

Noros conjured a final yelp as his brain exploded inside his skull, popping his eyes from their sockets. And with a final bloody gurgle, Noros the Lesser fell silent.

Raena released her mental grip and the lifeless body crumpled into the throne. The glow faded from her eyes and a grim stillness infected the chamber. She and Mireth stared at the corpse with a mixture of relief and anguish. The tyranny had ended, but the real work had only begun. How does one restore trust from the shadow of malice? That was a task for tomorrow.

"What do we do with him?" Mireth said.

"He wanted to be remembered," Raena said, then turned to a soldier. "Toss the body onto the palace steps. I trust the people will construct an appropriate tribute."

The soldier nodded, then approached the body. With a mighty hoist, he tossed the former emperor over his shoulder and turned for the exit. A satisfied grin stretched across his face as he walked the path of carnage into a new era.

THE END

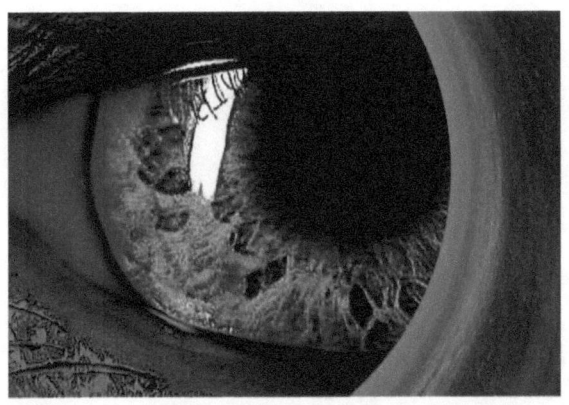

Horrible secrets lurk in the howling void.

In 2078, NASA created a wormhole portal and used it to colonize the solar system. When the United States collapsed, one of the gates was banished to deep space. The public forgot. But now a lonely caretaker will confront an existential terror.

THE EYES OF OWEN

Jesse stood inside the lobby of the Houston Space Command, wearing a gleeful smile. The relics of glory were scattered all around him. To his right, a scout drone from the Ceres mission of 2145. To his left, the famous Fido suit, which allowed the first dog to join a Mars colony in 2214. There was even the awe-inspiring photo from Voyager 8 when it overtook Voyager 1 in 2383. He studied them all with a giddy fascination. It was a big day, after all. He was joining a pantheon of greatness.

At least, he was trying to.

"Mr. Talbot?" said a voice from behind.

Jesse flinched and spun to the source, finding a young woman of a similar age. She wore a tailored suit with a NASA pin on the lapel.

"Yes. That's me. Hello." He extended a hand.

"Sorry to startle you," she said, completing the shake. "Ms. Landry will see you now."

"Ah, good. Yes. Um. Thank you." His cheeks puffed with a hasty breath.

"This way," the woman said with a warm smile, finding his nervousness endearing. She turned and walked towards a nearby door.

He followed her into a long and well-lit corridor. Clouded glass lined the walls with several office doors to either side. Their heels clacked along the tile floor, sending sharp echoes down the passage. After a short walk, the woman strolled to a stop and knocked on a door.

"Come in," said a muffled voice.

The woman opened the door and stepped aside, allowing Jesse to enter. He walked into the office of a dedicated professional. A lot of shelves, a lot of knickknacks and accolades, and most importantly, a director plaque resting atop a large wooden desk. The woman sitting behind it was firmly middle-aged and stout in figure. Her mission days were long over and she had embraced an office life.

"Mr. Talbot," she said without getting up. She gestured to a pair of receiving chairs in front of the desk. "Have a seat."

Jesse continued forward. The young woman closed the door behind him and vanished back into the hallway. He claimed a chair and lowered into the cushion with a touch of awkwardness. "It's an honor to meet you, Ms. Landry. I have studied all your missions."

"Mhmm." Her face was steeped in apathy.

"I was especially enthralled by your exploits on Europa."

"This isn't a fan club, kid."

"Yes. Sorry." His shoulders slumped a bit.

"Anyway," she said, lifting a tablet for study, "I reviewed your profile. And I must say, you are terribly overqualified for this position."

His smile faded.

"You have the chops to run an entire lab," she continued. "And for a *lot* more money. This is more of a babysitting gig. You get that, right?"

Jesse squirmed a bit, then stiffened his posture. "Yeah, but ... it's babysitting the greatest technological achievement in the last millennium."

"Maybe once," she said, adding a sigh. "Nobody cares anymore."

"I care." The statement was bold and confident. "The Eyes of Owen. Discovered in 2078 by Lindsey Owen, a NASA fusion engineer. Discovered by accident, in fact. The unintended and unreplicated results of a particle containment experiment. She called it a 'priceless mishap' because the portals were instrumental in colonizing Mars and terraforming Titan. During the second Callisto mission, they—"

"I get it," Landry said, raising a hand. "You're a fan."

"More like a dedicated enthusiast," he said with a half-smile, then paused for a moment of serious reflection. "You have a wormhole portal inside this building. And the sister portal is on a crewless ship 1.4 quadrillion kilometers away. Quadrillion, with a Q. I don't care that the public lost interest a hundred years ago. I don't care that deep space is desolate and boring. The Eyes of Owen remain utterly spellbinding to me. They are a testament to our curiosity and triumphs as a species. And I think that it's only right that someone with that reverence is the one who manages their upkeep."

Landry cracked a smile. "How long did you practice that?"

"All week."

They shared a polite laugh.

"Well, seeing as how you're the only one who applied, you're hired."

"Oh," he said with a deflated tone.

"I thought you'd be happy."

"I am." The disappointment in his fellow humans was hard to mask, but he snapped back to an eager demeanor. "I am. Yes. Thank you so much."

"Okay then." Landry rose from the desk. "Let's get you to the control room."

"What? Now?"

"One of our caretakers retired two weeks ago. I've been filling the role since then, and not to undermine your zeal, but I've got better shit to do."

A toothy grin stretched across his face. "Yes, ma'am!" Jesse shot to his feet and followed her out of the office.

* * *

The control room was on the first sublevel and enjoyed the security protocols of a mid-tier restaurant. That is to say, not much. In their heyday, the Eyes of Owen were widely regarded as critical assets. They were defended with the same fervor of a nuclear arsenal, given their ability to transport goods (and weapons) from one side of the planet to the other in the blink of an eye. This became doubly important when one of the portals was flown to Mars to help build the first settlement. For a hundred years, they captivated the minds of every human being.

Every mind, good and evil.

When the United States collapsed, the Texas Republic was besieged by those who wished to control the portals. NASA, now an independent organization, decided the best course of action was to launch one of the portals out of the solar system. They constructed a drone ship with ionic drives capable of reaching a quarter of the speed of light. A decade later, the portal was in deep space. And thus, worthless to any nefarious actors.

Once the dust had settled, the Eyes of Owen served a new purpose. It became a bucket list item for wealthy tourists. Rich schmucks with cash to burn were more than willing to fork over absurd bounties to see the big black empty. NASA made a killing, which allowed it to restore its place in the frontiers of space. But the unfortunate thing about the big black empty is that it's big, black, and empty. Celebrities lost interest and wealthy tourists flaunted their cash elsewhere. The portals faded from public consciousness and became a footnote in NASA history.

Centuries later, one portal resided in Houston Space Command, and the other continued its aimless plunge into deep space. Their significance forgotten, their legacies a grim reminder of humanity's inability to coexist.

Even so, none of it deterred Jesse.

He walked into the control room with the elation of falling in love. A short foyer led to a spacious chamber in the shape of a half-circle. Several tiers of stations rose from the base, like a small amphitheater. Each station controlled a different aspect of portal maintenance. Most required little attention, as the need for larger teams was deprecated long ago. The in-house AI handled most of the upkeep, but the physical presence of a human caretaker was still deemed necessary. The entire role was boiled down to a "just in case" contingency.

A single staircase split the stations down the middle, leading to a platform at the base. And there, pressed against the far wall, was a vertical rectangle with a deep purple glow. The portal was six feet wide, nine feet tall, and clung to a slab of tungsten a full foot thick. It menaced the space, but did not make a sound. The light within churned like a cauldron, creating a potent mix of fear and fascination.

"Bring a coat next time," Landry said, anticipating the chill that crept over Jesse's body. Given the heat from the stations and the lack of human activity, the room was kept cold. Not enough to see your breath, but enough to make a long stay uncomfortable.

Jesse barely noticed. He followed Landry down the stairs while pulling his widened gaze around the room. The stations blinked and chirped as data flowed through the system. Giant ducts hummed overhead as they recirculated the sterile air. The main showpiece was the portal itself, which grew larger and larger as they approached. Before long, it loomed over them like a hungry predator.

"Atmo check," Landry said.

A robotic arm detached from the wall, swung around to the portal face, and inserted a thin metal probe. After a few seconds, a trio of indicators turned green, denoting stable readings of temperature, gravity, and atmosphere. The probe retracted and the arm reset.

"Okay then, let's go." Landry walked towards the portal.

"Whoa, wait, what? We're going inside?"

Landry sighed and turned to Jesse. "You have to do this every day, son. Best get used to it." She pointed at the probe. "Just be sure to do that beforehand. We don't need you strolling into a decompression like a jackass. This position is hard enough to fill as it is." She turned away and stepped into the portal with a casual stride. It swallowed her without much fuss. A thin yellow band outlined her body as she passed.

Jesse gathered his wits and took a few stuttering steps towards the portal. Summoning the courage, he lunged at the glowing pane as if to welcome an unknown fate. The transition was instant, painless, and somewhat disappointing. He stood inside another control room, albeit a smaller one without physical stations. Numerous ports and panels filled the walls of the square chamber. The ceiling was much closer, matching the height of the portal, which was now behind him. He turned to face it. Still mesmerized, he lifted a hand and pushed it through the surface. It vanished back to Earth, drawing an involuntary gasp.

"The thrill wears off quickly," Landry said.

Jesse yanked his arm back and turned to find Landry standing in the center.

"It's strange to say that something so incredible can get so mundane." She sighed and glanced at the walls. "But it does."

Jesse started to respond, but couldn't find the words.

"Anyway," she continued, "let's get started. We're in the nerve center of the portal ship. Given your education, I would assume that you see many familiar components."

"Yes," he said and joined her at the center. He quickly scanned the room while pointing at the wall sections. "Diagnostics. Power. Navigation. Oxygen. Everything a healthy ship needs, minus food stores."

"Good. No food allowed, by the way. This is a clean transport and I want to keep it that way. No bathrooms either, so piss beforehand."

"Understood."

"So yeah, whatever the ship needs, run it through the portal. Supply lines are back in the main control room. I doubt you'll have much to do. After hundreds of years, the ship has been optimized to oblivion. The most common task is running lines for scans and data dumps, which the home system will prompt you for."

"Yes, ma'am." His eyes lowered in a sheepish manner, as if building up courage to ask her out. "If you wouldn't mind, can I, um, see it?" He gestured towards a lonely door that led to the rest of the ship.

Landry shrugged. "Sure. Knock yourself out." She pointed at the portal. "I'm gonna get some coffee. Meet me back in my office when you're done and we'll finish your onboarding."

"Yes, ma'am. Thank you."

She moseyed back through the portal, leaving Jesse alone on the other side of the cosmos.

The reality of the situation slowly consumed his thoughts. He had been alone before. He knew what isolation felt like. But never in his deepest, darkest dreams could he have imagined the howling dread of being truly alone. Jesse was a few steps away from comfort and safety, but light-years removed from his entire species. It penetrated his mind like a thousand needles. His entire nervous system was flooded with an otherworldly detachment.

But it was also intoxicating.

He exhaled a fluttering breath, then turned for the door. His cautious steps echoed inside the chamber as he approached. The door slid open automatically, revealing his first view of the great cosmic void. An observation hallway encircled the ship like a promenade deck, giving visitors a panoramic view of deep space. He stepped into the passage with his eyes fixed on the viewport. It was a few meters tall, filling most of the wall. Jesse trembled as he approached the pane and pressed a hand to the surface. It was cool to the touch. And beyond it, an endless sheet of stars. No sun, no moon, just nothingness in its full and terrifying glory.

His dangling jaw stretched into a wide smile.

Jesse pulled away and followed the black sheet around the entire passage. The twinkling dots were entirely foreign to his eyes. No familiar constellations. No planets or moons. No stations or satellites. He couldn't identify a star if his life depended on it. His mind embraced the void and traced new constellations, a menagerie of creatures known only to him. The minutes flew by as he devoured the enchanting vision.

As he strolled around the ship, he made a few interesting observations. First, the walkway was continuous. No cockpit or engine room to get in the way. The lack of a cockpit made sense, given the ship's autonomous nature. The ion engines, on the other hand, were a mystery. They must have been mounted vertically. An airlock was notably absent, or just well-hidden. Designs were kept secret during construction, for obvious reasons. But now that Jesse was a member of the team, he wondered if he had access to those juicy details.

A great question for Landry, he thought.

He grunted with embarrassment, realizing that she was waiting in her office. A hasty jog brought him back to Earth.

* * *

Jesse took to his new position like a duck to water. Over the next six months, he dutifully fulfilled his tasks while visiting the black beyond and loving every second. It was a dream come true. The ongoing mission to preserve the Eyes of Owen filled him with a sense of purpose, one that had been sorely absent from his life. He even started a relationship with the site manager, the lovely young woman who greeted his arrival. Her name was Camilla. She enjoyed Asian food and classic movies.

While not required, Jesse devoted his workdays to studying the various stations. He wanted to learn as much as he could about the miracle technology. In less than a year, he became the de facto expert in the entire solar system. His colleagues, despite earning the same wages under the same title, treated him as a project manager. Over time, their boredom morphed into curiosity. Jesse taught them everything they wanted to know, and in the process, turned them into proper researchers. Landry took notice and rewarded the team with raises.

As the assumed leader, Jesse enjoyed the day shifts. He worked five days a week from morning to afternoon. The other members divided the nights and weekends, with minor overlaps to share information. The only rule was that a human needed to be present in the control room. It was a flawless operation. The research expanded, the camaraderie grew, and the facility honored the team with a portrait in the lobby. It was unveiled with a modest ceremony. Jesse gave a short speech and cited it as the best day of his life. The next day, he proposed to Camilla, who tearfully accepted and bettered the previous day.

Life, as they say, was good.

* * *

The break room was stuffy that day, which sometimes happened when the climate system recalibrated. It was Houston, after all, so nobody complained. Dampness was baked into daily life. Jesse sipped on a mug of coffee while finishing a delectable snack. Camilla had found a fresh batch of sesame wafers at a local bakery, a rare treat. She gave some to Jesse before his shift, which brightened his day. He had relieved Sasha from the night shift an hour before, but couldn't wait for his usual break time. The wafers paired wonderfully with coffee, so he decided to enjoy them during a refill.

"How are they?" Landry said, poking her head in from the hallway.

"Incredible," Jesse said with a muffled tone. A few crumbs fell from his mouth as he crunched through the final wafer.

"I *just* missed them. Swung by the bakery yesterday and watched the last order walk through the door." She shrugged into a chuckle. "C'est la vie."

"Aw, that sucks. Sorry, I would have given you one a minute ago."

"Nah, more will come. Oh, and I just sent you the latest encryption protocols. Don't forget."

"I'm on it," he said, adding a thumbs-up.

Landry nodded and resumed her trek.

Jesse flicked some crumbs off his tie and rose from the chair. The metal legs squeaked across the tile floor as he reached for his jacket across the back. He found that a sport coat was the best weight for comfort inside the control room, which allowed a more professional style. He enjoyed dressing like a leader, and few would deny that he'd earned it.

He grabbed his coffee mug, a personal favorite that featured a cartoon cat complaining about Mondays, and refilled it on his way out the door. He merged into a steady traffic of engineers on their way to various parts of the complex. Meetings often spilled into walk-and-talks, so he was careful to avoid anyone with a distracted attention. The break room was near a stairwell, so he didn't have to contend with many bumped shoulders or spilled beverages.

A quick grab and yank opened the door. He slipped inside and hummed through a favorite tune as he descended to the sublevels. When he reached the next door, he bumped it open and spun into the hallway. Much less traffic, as the sublevels were home to long-term storage and special projects. The lights were dim and the air was crisp, like entering a hallowed den. He enjoyed it. The peace and quiet allowed for long stretches of concentration.

After a short walk, he leaned into the entry door of the control room. A rush of chilled air greeted his arrival. His ears welcomed the dull hums of the overhead ducts. His eyes welcomed the peripheral glow of the towering portal. He scanned some data panels along the path to the central stairs. All were nominal. As he turned to descend, he scuffed to a stop.

His eyes widened.

His chest swelled with fright.

There, looming over the lower platform, was a giant tentacle. Its fleshy mass was a meter thick and dripped with a cloudy mucus. A crooked tip hung like a shepherd's hook and snaked back to the portal plane. Several smaller tentacles clung to the rear wall, spreading out from the portal like a gruesome flower. They were deep red and pulsated like swollen veins. Some had wrapped around the basin and slithered atop the control stations. The room continued to blink and chirp, as if wholly oblivious to the intrusion.

Jesse whimpered.

The main tentacle whipped in his direction, like a cobra sensing prey. The entire mass began to rumble, creating ripples in the slime pool beneath it. The dull vibration crept around the space. Stations whined. Chairs wobbled. Ducts rattled overhead.

Fear consumed Jesse, but a strange paralysis kept him rooted in place. It pulsed inside his chest, then crawled up his neck and seized his mind. A guttural noise invaded his ears, like a distant horn in the mist. It grew louder and louder, rushing towards him with intent. His body tensed, bracing for impact. A wall of sound slammed into his conscience, creating a deafening shriek. His hands shot up to cover his ears. The coffee mug fell to the ground and shattered, spraying black liquid across the cold tiles. The shriek intensified, buckling his knees and pinching his eyes shut. He fell forward and tumbled down the stairs like a rag doll. His flailing body crashed at the base and writhed through the shrill invasion.

And then, silence.

Nothingness.

Jesse, still tucked and clenching his ears, unraveled from the knot and slowly opened his eyes. Another shriek, but this time from his own lungs. The tip of the tentacle was a meter from his face. He cupped his mouth and froze in place, awaiting an unknown fate. A dreadful stillness infected the room. Mucus dripped from the hide. Jesse remained pinned to the floor, panting with terror, eyes locked onto the mysterious beast.

Another sound crept into his mind. Not a horn. Not a shriek. Something more delicate. A voice. Or at least, an approximation of one. It formed a jumble of clicks, taps, and notes. More racket than chatter. However, some of it bore a hint of familiarity. A consonant. A vowel. And then, a word.

"Breed," it said with a deep and menacing voice.

"Wha—what?"

The voice did not respond. Instead, the tip of the tentacle began to convulse. It twitched and quivered before opening like a grisly flower. Mucus splashed onto Jesse, coating him with a foul stench as fleshy strips peeled back from the tip. No teeth, no tongue, not a mouth. Hidden inside was a black orb with a thin yellow slit across the face.

An eye.

It shifted inside and focused on Jesse. "You. Breed," the voice said again.

"Um," Jesse said with a quivering voice. His eyes scanned the interior, now crawling with deep red tentacles. It dawned on him that the creature had established a telepathic bond. It was hunting for intel, scanning for data. It was ... trying to communicate. "Breed? Me? You want me to breed?"

"No. You. Breed. Type."

"Oh, um. Breed. As in species?"

"Yes."

"I'm a human."

"Human."

"Yes, um, like a primate."

"Unfamiliar," it said after a brief pause.

"Uh," Jesse said, his voice still quivering. His eyes shifted back and forth as his racing mind struggled to make sense of the situation.

"Where," the voice said again.

"Where? Where what?"

"Galaxy. System."

"Oh, yes, um ... we call our galaxy the Milky Way. Our, um, solar system. It doesn't have a name, probably because we haven't discovered others. We call this planet Earth. I'm sorry. That, uh, probably doesn't help much."

"Hidden. Safe."

"I, um, guess you could say that. Yes."

A sudden clacking of footsteps caught the beast's attention. The yellow iris lifted inside the black orb, shifting its focus to the top of the stairs.

"Jesse, I forgot to tell you that—"

The clacking stopped.

Landry stood at the top of the staircase, wearing an expression of utter shock. Jesse angled his head to try and diffuse the situation, but before he could speak, another tentacle shot out from the portal and seized Landry's ankle. She yelped as it yanked her body into the air. And with a mighty whip, the tentacle sailed over the control room and slammed Landry onto the platform. Her skull exploded. Her body shattered. Blood sprayed in every direction from the devastating impact. It rained into the pool of mucus, creating a gory mosaic.

The tentacle, now dripping with human blood, also peeled back at the tip. But instead of another black orb, it regurgitated a sticky mass over the butchered body. It was cloudy, much like the mucus, but firmer, like an industrial glue. Numerous globs wriggled inside the mass. They palpitated like severed hearts. One by one, the globs burst to reveal squid-like creatures. Each one carried its own black orb. Their red tentacles wormed around the area, stretching and reaching with ravenous intent. They burrowed into the slaughtered flesh and began consuming Landry from the inside out.

Jesse swallowed a whimper.

"Quantity," the voice said.

Jesse stared at the carnage, unable to speak.

"Quantity," the voice said again.

His horrified gaze returned to the orb. "Of what?"

"You."

"Me. Of humans."

"Yes."

Jesse closed his eyes for a quick calculation, trying to ignore the warm brains and blood on his face. "18 billion, spread across two planets and some moons."

"Good."

"Good? How?"

"Offspring."

He glanced at the squidlings tearing through chunks of Landry. "Your babies? What about them?"

"Eat. Grow. Thrive."

The reality of the situation flooded Jesse's mind. His chest deflated and his shoulders slumped. The dripping blood faded into the background, leaving him face-to-face with a terrifying fate. In that deepest and darkest moment, he could only think of Camilla. "No," he said as a tearful plea. "Not here. Please."

The creature did not respond. Moments later, the black orb melted back into the tentacle. The opening widened as the mass lifted high into the air. Jesse could sense a dull rumble in the floor. It swelled with intensity. The tentacle flexed, as if to weather an intense burden. The rumble peaked with an explosion of cloudy slime. The tentacle whipped back and forth like a fire hose, spraying sludge on every surface. Before long, the entire room dripped with ooze. And much to Jesse's horror, countless globs squirmed within it.

The tentacle closed and hovered in the air, as if to survey its work. The other red tentacles began detaching from the room. They slithered back to the portal, leaving slimy trails in their wakes. Before long, only the big tentacle remained. It waited in silence as an army of tiny alien squids burst into existence.

Jesse pressed his back to the nearest station, his arms and legs slipping through the mucus. Several squids skittered across his body, but did not attack. He recoiled as their tiny tentacles gripped his flesh. A distant scream stole his attention. He peered around the station and up the stairs, where a single beam of light illuminated the entry.

His heart sank.

They were already inside.

Panic consumed him.

As he struggled to his feet, the tentacle wrapped around his waist and hoisted him into the air. Jesse flailed as the tentacle withdrew into the portal. The control room faded from view. A final scream echoed through the chamber as he departed Earth.

* * *

Moments later, Jesse stood inside the portal ship's nerve center, exactly where the tentacle had left him. He trembled with fear, unable to grasp the predicament. Ribbons of mucus dripped from his body, adding to the giant pool beneath his feet. His lungs struggled to inhale the foul air. It was thick with heat and humidity, an odd sensation given the location.

His gaze detached from the slimy floor and pulled itself around the enclosure. A throbbing red flesh clung to most of the interior, creating a cocoon of meat and muck. It also blocked the portal, preventing an escape. Data panels blinked through thinner sections, as if peeking through stretched skin.

A sudden movement caught his attention. He turned to find the tentacle resting in the lone doorway. The black orb had returned and the yellow iris studied him from afar. The viewport behind the tentacle was coated with the same throbbing flesh. After closer scrutiny, he realized that it was clinging to the exterior, as if the entire ship had been swallowed by a leviathan.

"I want to go home," he said to the orb.

The beast did not respond.

"Did you hear me?" His voice cracked with anger. "I want to go home."

"Cannot." The guttural voice penetrated his mind.

"Why?"

The flesh in front of the portal began to separate. It pulled apart, releasing wads of goo that splashed onto the floor.

Jesse gasped.

The purple glow was gone. The creature had shattered the tungsten slab, severing the wormhole. Countless cracks zigzagged across the surface like a broken windshield. It was lifeless, quiet, a simple stack of metal shards.

Jesse stepped to the broken portal and pressed a hand to the surface. The sorrow was more than he could bear. He wailed in agony as tears streamed down his face. He slammed his fists into the metal, over and over until the knuckles were bloodied. Panting and weeping, he turned to the black orb and pleaded for mercy.

"Kill me," he said softly.

The beast did not respond.

"Kill me!" he said again.

"No."

"Why not?! You stole *everything*!"

"Gift."

"Gift? What gift? What are you talking about?"

"Life."

Jesse paused in thought, then scoffed. "You son of a bitch."

"You. Help. Gift. Live."

"Live? *Live*?!" He struck the wall again. "I can't live without food and water! You've doomed me to a horrible death!"

"Time. Infinite. Death. Inevitable."

"Home! I want to go home! Send me home!"

The beast did not respond. Moments later, a chorus of squishing and sucking filled the room. The orb vanished into the tentacle and the interior flesh began to retreat. It seemed to bubble and dissolve like melting butter. Chunks detached from the ceiling and splatted onto the floor. They quickly disintegrated and slurped into tiny cracks. In less than a minute, Jesse was standing alone inside the control room. The mucus remained, but all traces of meat were gone.

He turned to the door and viewport, where the creature still clung to the hull. A morbid curiosity compelled him into the hallway. The tentacle was nowhere to be found. A dull rumble danced around the ship as the exterior flesh began to vibrate. Jesse steadied himself as the beast detached from the hull. The meat popped away like suction cups from glass.

The rumbles stopped.

The wall of flesh floated towards the bow of the ship. Jesse followed it up the hallway and stopped at the front, where the meat converged at a single point. He watched in bewilderment as the flesh pulled away from the ship and folded together like the petals of a massive flower. The creature turned slowly, like a giant ocean liner. Jesse could only gawk in disbelief as the goliath revealed itself. It resembled a hulking squid with countless tentacles, much like its offspring, but on a gargantuan scale. It was a living, breathing, spacefaring colossus. A true terror of the deep, but also a wonder of the natural world.

Jesse knew that the beast had burdened him with a slow and excruciating death, but he was also strangely moved. Humanity was doomed. Everyone he knew and loved was dying. But in that moment, he realized that life was stunningly resilient. Humans never stood a chance. They were tadpoles in a vast lake of horror.

"Okay then," he said, then turned away and shuffled back to the control room.

He wandered the room for a minute, then returned to the shattered portal. A hush enveloped the space. He examined the cracks with a fingertip, then lowered his gaze to the ground where a few shards had fallen. Reaching down, he grabbed one of the shards and lifted it for a ponder. It was the size of a steak knife with a jagged edge and sharp tip.

"Are you still there?" he said.

"Yes," the beast replied.

"Good. Fuck you and your gift." Jesse stabbed himself in the neck and slashed through an artery. Blood spurted from the wound as he crumpled to the floor. And there he lay, staring at nothing. A growing pool of red pushed the mucus away, a final act of defiance as the curse of life slowly departed his body.

THE END

Blind faith is a dark path to nowhere.

"The afterlife is real. We have proof." These seven words shocked the world and transformed the human condition. Ten years later, the research team has gathered for an anniversary interview. As a grateful planet watches on, something feels amiss.

THE OXFORD REVELATION

The interview set was awash in adoration. Wide smiles stretched across every face, from makeup artists to audio techs. The heroes of humanity were in the green room and a deep sense of gratitude had enveloped the staff. The four scientists in waiting were living legends, and the respect they carried was enough to guarantee the largest viewership the world had ever seen. In fact, the program running before the upcoming live feed had already eclipsed any event in history, based solely on anticipation.

A suited man exited a holding area and stepped towards the set. He was middle-aged with a sturdy frame and a gray, speckled beard. A pair of thick-framed glasses completed one of the most recognizable personas on the planet. Carter Nelson was the most respected journalist in the industry, hence his role as the interviewer. Ten years ago, he led the most important discussion in human history. And today, on this most auspicious anniversary, he would lead it again.

A pair of spotlights flanked a central wooden table. On one side, a single chair and a small stack of note cards. On the other, four matching chairs and pre-filled mugs of coffee. A bright backdrop with the network logo completed the stage dressing. Carter stepped onto the platform and took his familiar seat, prompting a makeup artist to rush in for touch-ups. There was no animosity, no snark or pomposity, just a pleasant exchange between two people.

"Thank you, Irene," he said as she finished her work.

"Dashing as always," she said, then tapped his shoulder and departed.

He turned to a camera operator, who was busy framing the shot. "Need me to adjust at all?"

"Nah," he said. "You're all good, Car."

Carter smiled and gave him a thumbs-up.

The studio, once a chaotic free-for-all that bent to time and pressure, was now a steady operation filled with competent and dedicated workers. It was a fellowship built on mutual respect. One might call it a family. Other networks had followed suit, creating a vibrant alliance that upheld news as a public service. Their shared commitment to bias-free reporting had recovered the public trust it had once abandoned. The Information Age created a monster of deceit, but it was The Oxford Revelation that slayed the beast.

"We're ready, Mr. Nelson," said a producer on the main floor.

Carter nodded and stood from the chair to signal his profound respect. He straightened his jacket and clasped his hands at his waist.

"Everyone," the producer said with a resonant tone. The staff halted and gave her their undivided attention. "Please welcome our special guests, The Oxford Four."

The entire room erupted with applause as the scientists emerged from the green room one by one. Vivian Gelb, a woman in her mid-50s with salt-and-pepper hair, led the pack. She smiled and waved at the adoring staff, many of whom had tears in their eyes. Paul Nguyen followed her, a slender fellow with a youthful demeanor. Melinda O'Brien was the third to emerge. Painfully shy, she could only offer meek nods. Brent Ramos was the fourth and final. He donned a toothy grin and immediately shook the hands of everyone he saw. His love of fame and glory was baldly apparent. But given the magnitude of the team's achievement, no one faulted him for enjoying the limelight.

They walked towards the central table, where Mr. Nelson was

waiting with a glowing smile. Vivian stepped onto the platform and greeted him with a firm handshake. They parted hands and she claimed the first of the four open seats. The applause continued as each scientist greeted the interviewer and took their assigned chair. As the guests settled, Mr. Nelson stepped to the edge of the platform and raised a hand, prompting silence on the set.

"Thank you very much, my friends," he said. "I am thrilled to share your kindness and solidarity on this glorious day, one that shall be remembered for many years to come. Your tireless work is greatly appreciated and my heart goes out to each of you. Please resume your preparations and let me know if there is anything I can do to help."

A dull roar replaced the silence as the crew returned to work.

Carter reclaimed his seat and expelled a grunt as his bum hit the cushion. Beaming with reverence, he eyed his guests like a proud father. "It's a fantastic honor to see you four again. Thank you, sincerely, for making the time to do this."

"The honor is ours," Vivian said.

The other three offered nods of support.

"It should come as no surprise," Carter said with a dignified tone, "but the viewership leading into this interview has already eclipsed every metric in television history. You will be, in a very literal sense, speaking to the entire world." He placed a hand over his heart. "A love like this is beyond compare, and I am grateful to be a part of it."

Brent smirked, enjoying the esteem.

Melinda maintained a nervous stare.

Paul nodded with appreciation.

"Thank you," Vivian said, adding a slight bow.

"30 seconds," said a crew member from afar.

A flurry of action consumed the set as everyone wrapped up their tasks and assumed their places. The guests cleared their throats and adjusted postures. Carter organized his note cards and brushed a piece of lint from his jacket.

"10 seconds," the crew member said, pulling Carter's gaze to the camera. A countdown clock appeared on the teleprompter. The final seconds ticked away and the live feed began.

"Greetings, citizens of the world," Carter said. "My name is Carter Nelson and I come to you with a special presentation. Ten years ago today, I uttered seven words that shook humanity to its core. 'The afterlife is real. We have proof.' These were, of course, not my own words, but the words of an Oxford scientist by the name of Vivian Gelb. She, along with her talented team, set out on an odyssey of mental inquiry. Their mission was to develop a visual representation of human thought, a live feed of cognition, if you will. What they discovered would change our world forever."

The camera view switched to the guests.

"I am joined today by those four scientists," he continued. "Vivian Gelb, Paul Nguyen, Melinda O'Brien, and Brent Ramos. The world knows them as The Oxford Four, and it is a distinct honor to have them with us today."

The studio erupted in applause again, mirroring a veneration shared across the globe.

"Thank you," Vivian said as the clapping faded.

"A pleasure," Paul said.

"Thanks," Melinda said.

"Great to be here, Carter," Brent said, adding a wink.

"The pleasure is ours," Carter said. "Ten years ago, you sat in these very same seats. You were unknown scientists, toilers inside a deep well of academia. Today, you sit before me as the saviors of humanity. Tell me, how have you managed this sudden and intense notoriety?"

"It's been a wild ride," Vivian said with a chuckle.

The other three echoed the sentiment.

"It's also been deeply humbling," she continued. "The single greatest impact on myself, and I imagine this is also true for my colleagues, has been a spiritual awakening. I started this journey as a neurologist. Learning how the brain works tends to undermine religiosity. You're not hostile towards it, you just begin to understand how the mind formulates belief. It was a curiosity, a phenomenon to study." She paused for thought. "Never in my wildest dreams could I have imagined myself as a true believer. But here I sit. I have become an advocate for the peace and love of the great beyond."

"That's beautiful," Carter said.

"I still call it God," Paul said. "I was raised in a Catholic household, but lost my faith shortly after leaving for college. Despite the non-exclusive nature of our discovery, there was a certain comfort in returning to my roots, so to speak. It restored my faith, albeit in a less structured manner." He chuckled into a sigh. "But yeah, like Vee said, the spiritual rebirth has been the biggest impact. I have been able to reconnect with my fellow humans in ways I never thought possible."

Carter turned to Melinda. "And what about you, Ms. O'Brien?"

She pursed her lips and lowered her gaze to the table, clearly uncomfortable with the attention. "Much the same," she said with a soft tone. "I was never in touch with anything growing up, divine or otherwise, so this was all new to me." She lifted her eyes to Carter. "To have that relationship now is a gift. But I do find it personal and hard to talk about, much to the chagrin of the press."

The group shared a polite chuckle.

"And you, Mr. Ramos?" Carter said, shifting focus.

"It's been a blast for me," Brent said with gusto, drawing a hearty laugh from the group. "I have loved every magnificent second. I get the best tables at restaurants, box seats at big games, and a whole lot of marriage proposals." He blew a kiss at the nearest camera, igniting more laughs. "But seriously, it's been a true blessing. I wouldn't change the last ten years for nothing. It's the honor of a lifetime to be part of this amazing movement."

"Speaking of the movement," Carter said, "let's go back to the very beginning. We all know the story, but it's a rare treat to hear it from the source. If you would be so kind, please refresh us on what you were researching that led to your monumental discovery."

"Sure," Vivian said, adding a sigh before launching into a well-rehearsed spiel.

"Ooo, I love this part," Brent said as he leaned forward onto his elbows.

More laughs followed as Vivian snorted with amusement. His comedic tone softened the obvious irritation of having to regurgitate the tale for the umpteenth time.

"I was researching perception," Vivian continued. "Brain waves, neural patterns, the whole gamut. But the problem was, I had no thesis. I was just researching for the sake of researching, which doesn't go over well in academic institutions. I needed to 'produce or perish,' as they say. So, after several polite scoldings, I got an idea. What if I could turn patterns into pictures? Just like a television. All it does is decode digital signals, so why couldn't I do the same with brain signals? The applications were endless, so I wrote and submitted a proposal. I was awarded a grant, which allowed me to put together a research team." She gestured to her cohorts.

"If memory serves," Carter said, "you and Paul are neurologists, but Melinda and Brent are computer scientists."

"Programmer," Melinda said. "On top of the medical research, the project had significant technical hurdles. That's why the proposal was for two neurologists, a programmer, me, and a systems engineer." She pointed at Brent.

"Brain movies take a lot of juice," he said.

More laughs.

"It was tedious work that often felt rudderless," Vivian continued. "It was all new. Just four people wandering in the dark. But then, after two long years, we had a breakthrough. Paul and Melinda isolated a few key signals that unlocked the neural network of a volunteer. It was like finding the mental equivalent of the Rosetta Stone. It allowed us to map the lot. Hopes, dreams, memories, nightmares, *everything*. The entire mental landscape opened up to us."

"Before long," Paul said, "we had a working prototype of a visual simulator. I will never forget the moment when we let our first volunteer, an older man, experience the device in real time. He thought of something, and there it was, living on the screen before his eyes. It was still grainy and glitchy, but it was there. He had lost his wife a few years prior and imagined a conversation with her. It was all there, and he wept."

The group shared a solemn silence.

"From there," Melinda said, "we were off to the races. Every day felt like a massive leap. We went from a glitchy mess to photo-real in six months. We could even translate sound."

"It was amazing," Brent said, "but the computational needs started sucking our budget dry. It was all hands on the panic deck. But then we demoed the device to the powers that be and *wow*, I have never seen funding replenish so quickly. Money rained on us like strippers at a frat party. It was *insane*!"

"A colorful analogy," Carter said with a hint of embarrassment.

"Sorry, I get excited." Brent shrugged at the camera and more laughs followed.

"Anyway," Vivian said, suppressing a snicker, "we finally had enough money to start planning for proper applications. The obvious targets were legal and medical environments, and it didn't take much convincing. For instance, a victim could synthesize memories of an accident, exposing critical details. A child could synthesize memories of trauma, giving doctors vital insights that the child cannot articulate. We called it Mind Sight."

"Were there any concerns for false positives?" Carter said.

"Yes," Paul said, "but the sheer amount of data that Mind Sight provided far outweighed the risks. Our clients fully understood that it wasn't an exact science. Memories can be faulty, but even bad ones reveal vast amounts of intel that would have otherwise been lost. Doctors have saved numerous lives by piecing together fractured memories." He paused for a weighted moment. "And it was in the hospitals where we uncovered the most astounding truth of our existence."

"How did that come about?" Carter said.

"Surgeons," Paul said. "Mind Sight provided a wealth of info during invasive procedures. Surgeons liked to keep a patient's thoughts on screen because it helped the anesthesiologists monitor distress. What they hadn't anticipated was that a non-zero amount of patients would die during procedures while linked to Mind Sight.

What they saw was ... shattering."

"An interesting word choice," Carter said.

"It's strong, but accurate," Paul said. "Death after death, they watched the foundations of reality shatter into a million pieces. The grand illusion, if you will, wholly unraveled."

"What did they see?" Carter said.

"Light," Vivian said. "Patients were engulfed by a warm and comforting light. But as you know, it wasn't about what they *saw*. It was about what they *heard*. Every dying person hears the word 'welcome' as they pass. Fourteen seconds later, the feed dies. Always fourteen." Vivian exhaled a measured breath. "That's when the soul leaves the body. True death."

"But you didn't know that yet."

"Correct," Paul said. "We had no idea what we were dealing with yet. As far as we knew, surgeons were getting spooked by a common dream state, and it's entirely common for people to have similar near-death experiences. But then the data started rolling in. For liability reasons, Mind Sight records everything when used in healthcare. What we found was, to put it mildly, unsettling."

"They were all the same."

"Yes, but also tailored." Paul lifted his hands and motioned in a circle. "Warm encompassing light, a voice saying 'welcome,' then fourteen seconds to black. But the thing is, the voice speaks in your own language. It has the same accent, the same inflections, the same nuance, perfectly catered to hit you with the most soothing and inviting tone possible. And at that moment, patients never show fear. Mind Sight scans have shown peace, elation, and contentment, but never fear. Every death we have ever recorded has ended the exact same way. Every sex. Every race. Every age. Every culture. Every creed. They all see the same thing, and it delights them. The data was overwhelming."

"And so we wrote a paper," Vivian said.

Carter grunted and smiled. "And that became The Oxford Revelation."

Another round of applause erupted from the set. The scientists glanced around the room, where countless watering eyes stared back at them. The exhilaration flooded the cameras and spread across the globe. A single proof had united humankind by answering the one question that plagued the mortal mind. They had solved the meaning of life, and the world rejoiced.

"I would like to turn to the aftermath," Carter said as the applause faded. "The Oxford Revelation sparked a worldwide crisis of faith. It was assumed that, given any disruption to a major religious force, violence would erupt. Were you surprised when it didn't?"

"Very much so," Vivian said. "In fact, that was our biggest fear. We debated releasing it at all, but given the subject, we knew the data would leak at some point. So, we thought it best to get out in front, regardless of consequence."

"Were you afraid for your lives?"

"Yes," Melinda said, prompting nods from the others. "I didn't sleep a wink the night before. I assumed there would be targets on our backs, especially from fanatics. That's why we peer-reviewed the paper into oblivion and why we insisted on a disclaimer. We wanted it known that the data did not affirm or deny any faith."

"That was a tense morning," Brent said. "It's a very weird feeling knowing that you have 'brought the good news,' but it might get you murdered."

"Thankfully, that wasn't the case," Carter said. "In fact, the praise was almost immediate, was it not?"

"Color me shocked," Brent said.

"Yes," Vivian said. "We received an outpouring of gratitude from hospitals and care facilities. That was key. We had the support of healthcare workers from top to bottom, which felt like a shield. The news spread quickly and we braced for impact. And much to our surprise, it never came. Instead, it created an aura, like a cocoon of solace. It was as if the entire world had paused to take a breath."

"Our civilization has changed a lot since that auspicious day," Carter said. "People are living lives of peace and prosperity. There is no war, no famine, no despair. The world has become an objectively good place. It feels surreal at times, like floating through a dream.

With that in mind, I have a question for each of you. What has been the most surprising outcome of your seminal work?"

A brief silence fell upon the table as the group contemplated.

"For me," Vivian said, "it would be the suicide industry."

The others nodded.

"It seemed to explode overnight," she continued. "And ironically, it was a direct result of the suicide taboo."

"In that religions frowned upon it."

"Correct. Religions have always viewed suicide as a mortal sin. They see it as a rejection of faith. This, unfortunately, created an enormous amount of needless suffering. Eventually, the pain is too great and attempts are made. Sometimes they failed, and those failures ended up in emergency rooms. Some died anyway, and those linked to Mind Sight still received the welcome message."

"There was one case," Paul said, "where a double murder-suicide was linked to Mind Sight. Surely this was an exception, right?" He shook his head. "Nope. He also got the message, and the implications were clear. No matter what you did in life, you were always forgiven in death."

"I remember this public debate," Carter said. "It created a massive cultural shift."

Vivian nodded. "The lack of cosmic consequence really galvanized the justice system. People do not like the idea that rapists, murderers, and psychopaths would escape punishment. So, in an effort to balance the scales, prisons shifted from holding cells to torture camps. Convicted criminals were held in isolation and denied death. In turn, medical advancements were focused on keeping prisoners alive for as long as possible. Today, the average age of inmate death is 175. That's the punishment, and it's a highly effective deterrent. Violent crime has fallen to a near-zero rate."

"The alternative being suicide."

"Right. Why commit a heinous crime out of desperation when you *know* that paradise awaits you at any given moment? Suicide became infinitely preferable, so much so that paid services became a huge part of popular culture. Want to die quietly in your home?

There's a service for that. Want to go out with a bang and throw a giant suicide party? There are *many* services for that. I saw one the other day that advertised itself as a virtual reality zombie apocalypse survival game." Giggles floated around the table. "I'm not kidding. Apparently, you get hooked up to a VR headset and try to survive a zombie horde for as long as possible. When you get caught, you get a sudden jolt that stops your heart. It's not my cup of tea, mind you, but I was astounded by the creativity."

"The craziest one I saw," Brent said, "was an LSD skydiving experience. No explanation needed. Just imagine falling from a plane, without a parachute, while tripping balls on acid."

"Colorful as always," Carter said.

More laughs.

"And what about you, Ms. O'Brien?"

Melinda bowed her head in thought. "The silence," she said after a long pause.

"How so?"

"The world has dimmed over the last ten years. And I don't mean literally, although that is true too. When we released the paper, nine billion souls were living on the planet. Today, it's less than four. Our work has directly resulted in the deaths of five billion people. It's a very difficult number to digest, even with the ethical clarity. I know we didn't murder all those people. All we did was prove that death wasn't final. I also look forward to seeing what's on the other side, but I can't shake the feeling that we disrupted something. I mean, who are we to be reapers?"

The table went quiet for a moment.

Sensing the mood shift, Melinda snapped back to a playful demeanor. "But then again, I sleep *really* well without car horns and angry pedestrians. Have you seen New York City these days? Zero traffic. It's wonderful."

More laughs as Melinda nudged Brent.

"Depopulation theory went out the window," Brent said. "That was the big thing I noticed. All the worries about economic impacts and demographic shifts just died on the vine. Removing the fear of death also removed the fear of aging. Nobody cares about fertility rates anymore. People live where they want and how they want. Life expectancies have actually gone up. The air is cleaner. The water is cleaner. Trade is more focused and fairer. It's like humanity finally pulled the stick out of its ass."

More laughs.

"Language, please," Carter said.

"My bad." Brent waved an apology to the camera. "I can't help it, I'm a giddy little cheerleader for this group."

Carter grinned, then shifted focus. "Mr. Nguyen, what say you?"

"Customer service," he said with a straight face.

The assertion drew side-eyes from the rest.

"Customer service?" Carter said, clearly confused.

"Yup. Everyone is so friendly now. When you remove the existential panic of everyday life, people just wake up in good moods. Think back to the before times when massive corporations offloaded basic customer service to bots and poverty wages. It was miserable for everyone. Now people work for pleasure and enrichment. You can't treat workers like crap when they have a ripcord to paradise. It killed the mega corps and created a boom for local businesses. The end result is a very happy and well-paid workforce."

"Same with education," Vivian said. "The students on campus are learning what they want to learn, instead of chasing degrees with the highest pay. It warms my heart to see a resurgence of the arts. Ten years ago, a music degree was worthless. Today, it's a viable career path. The cultural shift has been dramatic and fruitful." She paused for a moment of reflection. "It does make me wonder what I would have done. I don't know if I would have gone into neurology. I was staring down the barrel of massive student debt, and that affected my decision more than anything."

"Amen to that," Paul said.

Carter nodded with sympathy. "On behalf of all human beings, we are deeply grateful that you opted to become a neuroscientist."

"Thank you," she said with a half-smile.

Carter consulted his notes. "If it pleases the group, I would like to shift gears a bit."

"Fine with us," Vivian said, prompting nods from the rest.

"Thank you." Carter cleared his throat and took a measured breath. "I would betray my journalistic integrity if I did not address the proverbial elephant in the room. Over the last two years, your team has been accosted by a vile extremist group. You know of whom I speak, yes?"

"The Lumin Project," Paul said.

"I wouldn't call them vile or extremist," Vivian said. "They're misinformed, and given the nature of our work, I don't fault them for being vocal skeptics. Human beings have debated the meaning of life for thousands of years. It doesn't bother us at all."

"That's very charitable." Carter consulted a note card. "They have, in essence, asserted that your conclusions are baseless and your data is fabricated." He huffed and shook his head. "I applaud your compassion, but they spit in the face of anyone who holds your work in the highest regard. Thus, as the voice of our divine society, I would like to offer you a live rebuttal. Is there anything you would like to say to them now?"

Paul skirted the question and offered mundane anecdotes as Vivian's gaze wandered the studio. She remained calm, but her discomfort was beginning to show. Her eyes met with several crew members, all of whom gazed back with fervent adoration. After a brief search, she found her assistant standing beside an exit door. The assistant responded with a thumbs-up across her waist, making sure to keep the gesture hidden. Vivian replied with a subtle nod, then returned to the conversation.

"I would like to respond directly," she said, interrupting the exchange.

Carter stammered for a moment. "Pardon?"

"The Lumin Project. I would like to respond to them directly. Now."

"Certainly." Carter shrank back and cleared his throat. Addled by the assertion, he shuffled his note cards and gestured towards a camera. "The stage is yours. Whenever you're ready."

Vivian turned to her cohorts and nodded. In response, they rose from the chairs and disconnected their audio packs. One by one, they placed the devices on their seats and exited the stage, leaving only Vivian and Carter.

"What's happening?" he said.

Vivian ignored him and stared into the camera. "This is what I have to say to The Lumin Project." The world held its breath. Every eye was locked onto her face. "You're right. Our claims are baseless. Our data is fabricated. We bought our peer reviews and bribed every colleague to stay quiet, including Ben Lumin. It would seem that his conscience has finally caught up to him."

"Now wait a minute," Carter said, clearly flustered.

"It's a lie, Mr. Nelson," she said, turning to face him. "All of it. Every word."

"I don't—"

"There is no afterlife."

The sharp response drew several gasps.

Carter stared at her with mouth agape, stunned into silence.

Vivian sighed, then turned to address the camera. "Ten years ago, our society was on the verge of collapse. Resource depletion, hyperinflation, war, poverty, tyranny, famine, we endured it all. And then the oligarchs started buying water. *Water.* The essence of life, the one resource that nobody should own. Not you, not me, not a tech billionaire with psychotic delusions. That's not a savvy investment. That's a civilization staring into the grave.

"We knew that no politician was going to address the sustainability crisis. They're the ones who created it. They allowed corporate criminals to poison your food, pollute your land, and force you into lives of servitude. They raped your future for bigger yachts.

"So, we decided to fix it.

"The only viable solution was a rapid reduction in global population. Extreme, yes, but necessary. And most importantly, we needed you to *want* it. The entire human experience is driven by the fear of death. It is the source of our beliefs, our doubts, and our despair. If we were to succeed, we needed an impeccable answer to that impossible riddle.

"And so we wrote The Oxford Revelation."

Carter stuttered as Vivian stood from the chair. She unhooked her audio pack and tossed it on the table. Ignoring the cameras, she addressed the crew, all of whom wore faces of horror and dismay.

"We did it to save our species," she said, her words burrowing into countless ears. The cameras remained tightly focused on her face. "And by that metric, I think we succeeded. The truth was coming out, and I would rather you hear it from me. Hate us if you want. You're never going to see us again. But I implore you all to remember what you have built. You live in a miraculous world of peace, freedom, and fortune. Yes, it was built on a lie, but what world isn't? Perhaps this one is worth defending."

Vivian stepped off the stage and hurried towards her cohorts, who stood with her assistant near the exit. Without looking back, they slipped through the door and vanished from sight. The camera whipped back to the main table, where a shellshocked Carter stared at the surface. Tears rolled down his cheeks as the reality of the situation consumed him.

"I killed my own children," he said, then lifted his eyes to the world. "All they wanted was to see her again." He howled with agony and the feed cut to black.

THE END

ABOUT THE AUTHOR

Zachry Wheeler is an award-winning science fiction author. His many interests include photon hunting, full-contact chess, and vertical wit. He lives on Earth with his wife and cats.

Learn more at **ZachryWheeler.com**

If you enjoyed these twisted tales, please consider posting a short review. Ratings and reviews are the currency by which authors gain visibility. They are the single greatest way to show your support and keep us writing the stories you love.

Thank you for reading!

www.ingramcontent.com/pod-product-compliance
Lightning Source LLC
Chambersburg PA
CBHW022059170626
46808CB00002B/513